Dumped

Josef Peeters

Published by Arkturor Publishing

Author's web site:

http://lakesidecaravanpark.wixsite.com/josef

Edited by:

Sarah Farrugia

HEARTT Writing & Editing

cosmo12@bigpond.com / + 61 417 527 123

ISBN-13: 9780648456148

DEDICATION

To my wife, Sandy.

CONTENTS

Other books by the author

Fiction:
Daintree Denizens (thriller)
Mt. Moulamein (sci-fi)
Transience (magic realism)
Black Heart (psych. thriller)
Endure (dystopian) Out soon
Horror Series:
Eat What You Kill (Book 1)
B.A.M. (Book 2)
Eye For An Eye (Book 3)
The Guardians (Book 4) Out soon

Non-Fiction:
Wood Whisperer Volume 1
Wood Whisperer Volume 2
Wood Whisperer Volume 3
Giving Up (Short, autobiographical)

Visit Josef's web page for all purchase links and book descriptions;
http://lakesidecaravanpark.wixsite.com/josef

DAY ONE

When Mark opened his eyes he was blinded by the remorseless sunlight, reducing his pupils to pinpoints. Then pain abruptly made its presence known. Peering downwards, he could see his right leg bent in a shape that was not normal for a leg. His breathing was laboured due to severely bruised or broken ribs.

When his eyes finally adjusted to the glare enough to squint, he discovered that he was in his seat, alone, outside the plane, on a beach! He saw no sign of the plane, or Louise, or anyone else. He remained securely fastened to the seat by the cinching seat belt, with his leg broken below the knee. Footprints led away from the seat into the distance.

He screamed in agony as he attempted to move. The screaming caused his chest to hurt and his brain felt like it was about to explode. The row of seats on which he sat, rested on the lower section of the beach, with waves lapping at the edge. He was soaked through, and despite the heat from the sun, felt a cold deep within his marrow.

Another minor pain reminded him that his seat belt (which probably saved his life), was biting painfully into his lower gut. Slowly, he straightened himself further to relieve the pressure. It only caused extreme, white-hot agony to course through his system from the broken leg that flopped uselessly beneath him. It took several minutes for the waves of pain to subside enough for him to resume thought. While keeping his body as still as possible, he released the seat belt.

One less discomfort to deal with; dozens of others to go it seemed. He surveyed his immediate surroundings without turning his head. He had possibly been in a slumped position for a long time before he sat upright. A colossal headache was gradually ebbing, though not quickly enough for Mark's liking. He allowed himself to become concerned at his solitude, with only the mysterious footprints to suggest another presence.

He could not see behind him and had no intention of turning his head any time soon. While he felt like shouting for help, he didn't believe it would gain assistance or be heard by more than the ocean or the sand. No other sounds of human life were heard by him. He thought only to rest for a time, to gather himself and his thoughts, to run through what he knew.

Louise! He could remember the heated argument he was having with his fiancée before waking up on the beach. He remembered a white flash the moment before the lights went out.

***

"Ladies and Gentlemen, this is the Captain speaking. I apologise for the bumpy ride. To avoid the worst of the bad weather, we are descending to a lower altitude and skirting the edges of the unexpected storm cell. Unfortunately, this will delay our arrival time. The good news is that the weather in the Hawaiian Islands is unaffected by the storm with clear sunny skies and balmy temperatures. Should you have concerns about connecting flights, please inform one of the flight attendants who will notify the appropriate airlines to make other arrangements. Please remain seated whilst the seatbelt sign remains on. Thank you for your patience. We apologise for any inconvenience. Enjoy the rest of your flight."

Ignoring the captain's interruption to their argument, twisting uncomfortably in his seat to face Louise once more, Mark wrestled with his seat belt which seemed too tight. "Are you out of your mind? I mean, you can't be serious?" he whispered.

Louise nodded her head solemnly.

"If this is a joke, it isn't funny, Louise", Mark added. "How can you do this to me? To us? We're about to go on the holiday of a lifetime. We have planned and saved for this pre-honeymoon holiday for years. Halfway there, WHAM, just like that you tell me you're pregnant with someone else's child? What the fuck is going on? Why are you doing this? What have I done to deserve this?"

"Glad you finally asked. Don't think I didn't see you at the train station six months ago."

"Are you insane? What the hell does that have to do with anything?"

"Don't play that game with me, Marky-boy, I saw you clear as day."

"I am trying as hard as I can to stay calm and keep my voice down here but I will lose it soon if you do not explain what that horseshit means. I have no idea what you're talking about, and you know I hate that name you always come up with when you're pissed off about something."

"It's over, Mark, I saw you at the train station when I went there to pick up, June."

"Wait a minute, June? That day when you went to the city for drinks with, June? You're saying you saw me at the same train station?"

"Catch on quick don't you?"

"Sarcasm does not become you, *dear*. I still don't understand what this is all about even if you did see me that day."

"Oh, come off it, I saw you. No need to deny it. When I saw you there, I knew it was over for us. How could you do it? I never cheated on you!"

"Didn't you just tell me you did? That you're carrying someone else's baby? That you will meet this person when we land, to have a holiday with *him* while leaving me stranded?"

"Well, sure. After what I saw that day, I started seeing Luke. At least I knew he wanted me and only me."

"Luke? What, no, Luke Harman? Now I know you're kidding around, but it's a shitty thing to do, Louise."

"I'm not kidding, I'm seeing your friend, Luke. You practically drove me into his arms."

"He is not, and never was, my friend. Are you going to tell me what you think you saw or do I go on guessing what it's all about until we land? When I finally give that slime ball his just desserts."

"Do that and we call the cops."

"You think I care? It would be worth going to jail to see him sprawled on the tarmac. How could you have hooked up with *him* of all people? Makes me ashamed to have ever been your partner if your taste in men is that bad! You two deserve each other and I hope he treats you like I know he will. Did you know he was into swinging? And both ways might I add."

"What does that mean?"

"Multiple partners, any gender, dear. I hope you were careful…oops, no you weren't. Gee, wonder what diseases you will catch? What will you give to the bastard you're carrying?"

"Jealous, Marky?"

"Confused, Louise, not to be mistaken with jealousy by any stretch of the imagination, and counting my lucky stars I find this out before our wedding. I, I… fuck! I can't believe how callous you are to do this. What did you think you saw?"

"You honestly can't remember? You do it that often that you can't even remember that incident?"

"I have done nothing at all, let alone often. Can you please just tell me straight? What is it I'm accused of?"

"I saw you with her; that…prostitute! Right there on the platform for all the world to see. Hugging and kissing and twirling around like long lost lovers. The familiarity you displayed was evidence of an on-going arrangement. I was so ashamed that you felt you had to pay for sex while you had me at home anytime you wanted. I felt dirty and used. You talk about diseases, what about the filth they sleep with, passing on to you and God knows who else? Didn't you think something was wrong when I refused to sleep with you after that day? No way was I going to catch anything from you, so I accepted an invitation from Luke to go out the following week. We've been seeing each other ever since and you don't understand what you are talking about when it comes to

Luke. He isn't into other partners and certainly not male partners."

Mark sat there for a long moment absorbing the information as the plane droned on toward the island destination intended as their dream come true. He scoured his memory to find the day at the train station she mentioned, the day she went to pick up June. She told him in the morning at breakfast that she was going to the station at lunchtime to pick up her best friend. They would do lunch and shopping in Chapel Street afterwards. She asked him… what? Something about joining them at lunch? Prostitute? Mark had never…shit! Okay, okay. Shit, he supposed she was right to be shocked if she saw that.

"It wasn't at all what you thought. Why wouldn't you ask for an explanation?"

"I didn't need an explanation, I saw it with my own eyes, and, June saw it too."

"You don't understand…"

***

Mark remembered the bright flash. Lightning? Possible, he thought because they were trying to get around a storm system at the time. Bomb? Surely not with all the bullshit going on since 9/11. A surface-to-air missile like the one that shot down the plane over that Russian place? Hard to be sure as he didn't even know the plane route or what landmasses they would be flying over. His geography sucked big time, so he had no idea where he might be other than somewhere in the Pacific Ocean. They may not even be anywhere near the air route anyway, seeing as the captain said they were deviating from their normal path.

Who knew how long the plane remained in the air after he blacked out. Did the pilots get off a mayday call? Is the black box, which is really orange, nearby to lead rescuers to his location? Castaway? Impossible. Yet he was alone on an island. He was glad there were no volleyballs nearby for him to begin talking to.

There were no storm clouds. No clouds at all in a clear blue sky with a brilliant orb bestowing inhumane temperatures and light intensities upon the earth. Ahead of him, all he saw was an endless expanse of beach with waves rolling gently in perpetual motion.

Higher up the beach, he spied the ubiquitous coconut palms dotting the dunes. Under any other circumstances, an idyllic setting in paradise. The agony he endured reminded him that this particular paradise was tainted. Not only was he at the mercy of the elements and the unbelievable pain assaulting his body, but he was also entirely isolated.

After taking in as much detail as possible of his surroundings, Mark knew that his first order of business was going to have to be attending to his broken leg. He was certain he was in for a world of hurt if he moved but knew he could not remain in the seat for much longer. Sooner or later the tide would turn and he would be caught by the advancing waters. He knew he would have to face incredible pain to move beyond the high water line.

He had to find some way of splinting his leg before more damage or internal bleeding occurred. He checked his pocket for the paracetamol capsules that were there for the earaches flying caused him. He wished earaches were his only concern at present. The packet was still there with only two of twenty-four capsules missing. He punched out three which he swallowed with difficulty due to his dry throat. He realised he would need fresh water before too long as well.

Who knew how long he had been in the water and how much seawater he had swallowed before he woke. His watch was of little use as it was totally water-logged. The sun was high in the sky which meant it was around midday. The plane left Melbourne airport at around five in the morning. They had been at least seven hours into their eleven and a half hour flight across the Pacific, which meant it could no longer be the same day. Was that the name of the damn ocean? He wished he knew more, that he'd paid better attention in geography classes at school.

As far as Mark knew, there had to be quite a few islands along the flight path, though he could not be sure. He could not know how long the plane remained in the air or what direction it was flying at the time he blacked out.

He doubted that it was the same day of his flight, it had to be the following day. It would only be a matter of time before rescuers scoured the area along the flight path to find survivors, if they weren't already. He didn't panic about being found. He only worried about his condition, when he was eventually found.

To stay alive until then meant he had to prioritise. Leg first, thirst, hunger, and shelter later. He knew that the warmth of the sun would dry his clothes soon enough, so he scanned the upper beach area for anything that might help him set his leg. There was an overabundance of driftwood to choose from littering the high watermark.

He could make out some frayed hawser among the flotsam and jetsam scattered throughout the driftwood. He thought he may be able to unwind the hawser to retrieve manageable rope lengths with which to tie the splints to his leg. He could not plan anything beyond that task as he would most likely blackout from the pain a few times in between. The pain capsules would only take the edge off, nothing more. He gritted his teeth to prepare for the ordeal.

The first blackout occurred not long after he moved off the airline seat. The searing, relentless pain continued to plague him throughout his crawl to reach the driftwood. He screamed at the top of his lungs each time his foot caught on a lump of disturbed sand or seaweed. Mark could not imagine torture at the hands of an enemy during wartime being any worse. Thousands of POWs might argue that point, however. He was in no mood to debate the issue, though thinking of useless shit like that distracted him from the intensity of the pain.

He was unsure how often he blacked out during his crawl, it just felt like an eternity before he reached his goal. It didn't take him long to find suitably sized sticks with which to splint his leg. He began untwisting the large hawser into manageable strands of sufficient length. Once the rudiments of his first aid were gathered, he faced the next problem of aligning the two broken pieces.

He would have to stretch his lower leg to a point where the bones straightened. To accomplish that task would mean anchoring his foot somehow and stretching the leg.

Mark had no idea if he possessed the courage to achieve his goals involving pain on such a scale. He knew he had to try, otherwise, his leg would never knit and would probably require amputation. Amputation may well be necessary regardless of his efforts, but that didn't mean he shouldn't try. He steeled himself for the expected outcome. Placed his foot between two large driftwood trunks nearby, then pulled back suddenly and hard.

When he woke, the sun was well down on the horizon. He prayed fervently that he succeeded the first time around because he seriously doubted his ability to repeat the procedure. He peered down at his leg. It was as good as he believed he could manage without better equipment at his disposal. The pain of securing the splints to four sides of his leg didn't begin to compare to the previous manoeuvre.

He pushed another three capsules out of the packet. He would have to ration them to conserve them as long as possible. Eating and swallowing the capsules was getting harder the dryer his throat became. Water would become his next priority rapidly. He didn't know how long he could last without water. A couple of days tops? He didn't know how long the rescue would take, but he was determined to be alive when it arrived.

The night air would get cool, no doubt. It meant he needed to find somewhere to hole up for the night which was fast approaching. Exposed as he was on the top of the beach was not an option despite his recently dried clothes. From his low vantage point, he was unable to make out much beyond the dunes at the top of the beach, but he could see some low shrubs which he may be able to slither under for protection. He would need some crutches to get around with, but that would have to wait for the next day.

After the pain he had caused himself, he would need to convalesce, gather his strength for the days to follow. He hoped there would not be too many to endure before help arrived. He was strangely calm considering his predicament. Panic never helped him in the past, so he didn't think it would assist him in his present circumstances. He mustered his remaining strength for the task of moving himself beyond the dunes to find some shelter.

***

Mark gasped in awe at the panoply of stars visible that night. He lay just beyond the overhanging branches of shrubbery atop the crest of the dunes, staring up at the magnificent display, impossible to be seen through the ambient light of most cities. It had been a very long time since he had been camping. He moved from the country to the city of Melbourne to follow his career at the age of eighteen. After his younger brother Frank passed away from his final bout of cancer, leukaemia, Mark could not remain at home.

He and his brother would often go off together camping beside different creeks, rivers and lakes around central New South Wales when they were younger. Then cancer came, which ate away their time, their happiness and his well-being.

He had not been camping since. It would not have felt the same without Franky there, so he didn't bother. He ran away to the city at the first opportunity to become a lawyer. He had visions of nobility like any other young student lawyer, which quickly disappeared. He was a public defender with Legal Aid and his clients were almost always guilty.

Mark represented the lowest of the low and he hated every moment. He was on the verge of changing jobs, trying to go it alone. He was waiting to talk Louise around after their holiday. He shook his head at the thought of his fiancée. Mark could not believe the stupidity of her actions. Had she just asked him about the meeting at the train station she would have understood.

He didn't even know if Louise had survived. Were they her footprints he saw? Surely she wouldn't have just abandoned him like that? Not that he really cared after what she revealed. For her to throw away everything they had worked towards over a misunderstanding, astonished Mark no end. He could definitely see how she might misconstrue what she had witnessed, but to assume so much without a word, then throw herself to that…thing, Luke, was unforgivable.

The premeditated revenge of dumping him on their way to Hawaii was the lowest act imaginable, only to be capped off by the revelation of a pregnancy to that lowlife prick! Mark seethed silently when he thought about them sneaking off. He started piecing together the snippets he recalled that didn't ring true at the time. The night she stayed over at a friend's place. A look of evasion when he asked about her evening. Her reluctance to make love of late and so many other moments that began to make sense in the light of the new knowledge.

How naïve he had been not to question her further when her answers didn't gel, when timelines didn't marry, when she was out more often than reasonable. He figured their jobs were causing them to drift apart slightly; he hoped that the vacation would remedy that. They were going to work out their wedding date on the trip, discuss arrangements, and make preparations.

Despite the problems they faced he never once imagined they were insurmountable. Mark believed she was the one for him, for better or worse. Luckily he found out the worst before they tied the knot. Not that he was such a traditionalist that he would not have considered divorce in the event of a revelation like an infidelity.

He was just glad that he didn't have to go through the orchestrations of divorce on top of the heartache. Mark had been involved in far too many divorce proceedings through his job without having to deal with his own.

He didn't feel an overwhelming sadness at having lost Louise as a partner, nor did he feel any grief at the possibility she may be dead. He was, if anything, angry. More than angry, he was furious. How dare she humiliate him like that? Louise obviously loved him very little, if at all, to be capable of such a premeditated act. To be having an affair with that creep for nearly six months!

That was the thing that made him more irate than anything else. To be sleeping with the man, possibly in their shared house, made him quake with pure fury and disgust. To think, that the mongrel had defiled the woman he loved, made him physically ill. Or maybe it was just the fact that he hadn't eaten anything all day, except pain killers.

He was bone-weary. He didn't think he would get much sleep because of the discomfort. He was wrong.

The following morning, Mark woke to the distant sound of engines overhead. He tried to scramble clear of his meagre cover as quickly as his leg would allow but knew all too well how futile the effort would be. He would be a small speck on a seemingly large landmass, with no way of attracting the attention of a passing plane. He needed a signal fire, or an SOS spelled out on the sand or something other than some feeble arm-wave from among the foliage.

No one would see him, but at least he knew they were searching. It was a good sign. He would have to gain some form of mobility in order to investigate his surroundings. Mark desperately wanted to find other survivors, to pool resources and ideas with them, to find a way to attract a rescue and survive. He risked increased pain attempting to walk around with improvised crutches but saw no alternative.

The island may be huge, at least, huge enough for someone on foot trying to circumnavigate it. Water was also on top of the list. Without water, despite the presence of coconuts, his chances of survival remained very slim. It may be days before the plane's return. He would have to be ready for them. He would have to have a plan, make fire…something!

He manoeuvred himself to the crest of the dune once more to survey the scene in the morning light. With the splint tightly in place, the struggle to move was made more bearable. It still hurt like a son-of-a-bitch, but bearable. He spied a few likely pieces of driftwood from his perch. Whether they would be the correct length he could not ascertain until he was down there. He slithered down the dune on his rump, careful to avoid his leg snagging anything on the way down. He managed to find a reasonable pair of sticks with Y sections on the top to cradle beneath his armpits and another protrusion lower down to act as a handle.

Mark opted to use the firmer sand near the water's edge to make the attempt rather than risk the soft sand of the dunes or the interior. The sand seemed to go for some distance beyond the dunes he noticed, after sheltering beneath the shrubs. The weight of the splints made hard work of keeping his leg off the ground, causing him to stop frequently.

Thankfully there were few obstacles to negotiate on his way. The heat made its presence known as the sun ascended. He would have to stop before too long as he was sweating profusely. Loss of bodily fluids would hasten his demise if he wasn't careful. He had to find water but thought it an impossible task if he was unable to go inland. He looked once more beyond the dunes to a seemingly impenetrable interior of dense foliage.

He could discern no hills or raised earth from which to survey the island. He had spotted many palms with coconuts on either the ground or the trees. Trouble was, a way to break into them, without any discernible means of doing so. Along the beach, in the distance, he saw some rocks protruding from the waves and up the shoreline, and...movement? It was too hazy to define any shapes accurately, so he staggered on as best he could, biting down hard on the pain the effort produced.

As he neared the shimmering rock formation he saw something bobbing on the gentle swell and more movement from the shore. He could not hasten his pace as his energy reserves were practically nil and the pain was excruciating. He had downed several more paracetamol to stave off the worst of it but felt it achieved little. The longer he struggled on, the more often his beleaguered leg dropped, allowing the foot to touch the sand. Spasms of intense agony resulted. He didn't think he could go much further. When he was close enough, he imagined he saw suitcases washed up on the shore and in the water among the rocks.

He realised it was not his imagination playing tricks on him at all. He recognised the floating objects and some of the scattered ones onshore as luggage and what he had thought were rock formations were actually more seats from the plane. Other debris had washed ashore as well, including a hostess trolley. The type of thing they wheel up the aisle with…

Could it possibly be? Could there still be drinks in there? Oh, Christ let there be a bottle or two left in there, he prayed. Anything, anything at all to drink, as long as there is something. He could not wait to get there, could taste the sweet water on his lips as he drew nearer. The movement turned into definable shapes. Animals. Pigs! Rooting around the seats and other objects.

They scattered reluctantly on his approach. The upturned stainless-steel trolley came into view. He nearly cried when he spied the vacant interior. Empty shelves, nothing! He cast about frantically trying to find a plastic bottle amid the suitcases, finally resting his eyes on a likely object.

It was almost buried in the sand, but it did turn out to be what he'd hoped. He unscrewed the bottle with great difficulty. With trembling hands, he lifted the bottle to his mouth.

Mark nearly spat out the contents in disgust when he recognised it as tonic water. He barely managed to keep it in despite the taste without the requisite tot of Gin. There was a smattering of other bottles washed up among the debris. Mark felt his stomach revolt as he spied the human remains on and near the seats. It was clear to him then what had attracted the pigs.

Partial corpses lounging on seats twisted out of shape. Large chunks removed from the seats and the cadavers from sharks and other sea creatures before the tide receded to be further destroyed by feral pigs. Traces of blood still draining away from the scene, diluted by the tide. Pink froth gathering at the shoreline amid clothing and body parts. Crabs and seagulls fighting over the spoils. Mark turned to the side and vomited. His stomach could not hold it in with so much gore about him.

As much as he wanted to escape the area, to avoid the horrible sight of human devastation, he knew he had to explore the luggage in an effort to find anything useful. He detested the thought of going through someone's personal belongings, especially with half of that someone still there, but he knew it was imperative to his survival.

An hour later, he stumbled off, leaving the carnage behind. He found several useful items which he had secured in a backpack he donned to continue his journey. Extra clothes of course, including a hat, sun lotion, and lots of it. Apparently, people did heed the cancer warnings because nearly every piece of luggage contained a bottle or tube of sun cream. Nail clippers which included a concealed folding knife would come in useful. How the little implement managed to get through the detectors he didn't know. It may have been packed in checked-in luggage rather than a carry-on. Either way, it was a boon not to be scoffed at.

He did find several more bottles of actual water. One tiny bottle of Vodka, one can of beer and in someone's carry-on, a packet of potato chips. He had hoped to find more water and some more edibles but was not disappointed with his haul. It would assist greatly. He didn't find the one thing he desperately hoped to come across, something with which to start a fire.

He assumed there might be more luggage further along the beach, as well as more corpses which he didn't look forward to seeing. He could do nothing for the ones he left behind as he didn't have the wherewithal to bury them. He assumed too, that identification would be necessary, making burial a non-option. Mark was immensely relieved to have quenched his thirst for the time being. Hunger would be accommodated with some potato chips or whatever else he may find.

Late afternoon saw Mark struggling to go any further. His leg was too painful to continue and he was simply exhausted. His leg had swelled to twice its normal size. He had seen no tell-tale signs of infection other than swelling. Constantly monitoring the colour, temperature and smell of his broken limb, Mark made his way along the beach.

He also kept a wary eye out for signs of previous occupation by himself or others. He didn't wish to keep circling the island indefinitely. If he saw anything remotely resembling footprints or other signs of life, he intended to follow the suspect spoor. He had not managed to find anything that day. At the top of the high water mark, Mark surveyed the bushes once more for a likely place of refuge from the cool night breezes.

He was no longer overly concerned about the cold as he had more than enough clothing and a small blanket to keep him warm. He did worry about the rain, though and considering it was a tropical island, rainstorms were a given. It was not a matter of if, but when, the rain would come and whether he could find or construct some shelter before then, or more importantly, some way of capturing the precious liquid.

He still needed to determine the dimensions of the island and explore it fully in the hope of finding more supplies, or better still, survivors in better shape than he. All in all, he was pleased with his progress. He had administered to his badly broken leg, found a few potentially life-saving items after trekking along the shore despite the pain involved in keeping his leg raised.

He didn't look forward to what he may find on the windward side of the island. As best as he could tell, he was leeward, on the protected side. He remembered reading about that somewhere. Then again he could be thinking absolute bullshit and simply be kidding himself into believing his hyperbole.

He had visited Orpheus Island in Queensland with his family one time and the difference between the two sides of the island was like chalk and cheese. The side facing toward the mainland was an idyllic calm-water island setting, while opposite, facing the open ocean was a wild and woolly affair of harsh rocky outcrops lashed by monstrous waves. Part of this island had to face the prevailing winds at some point unless the entire area was beset by the doldrums.

The journey to the sand dunes at the top of the beach was a hazardous task on crutches. If he wasn't mindful of every step into the soft sands, he would overbalance easily, causing more pain than he cared to imagine. His body needed rest after the arduous endeavours of the day.

The image of the corpses bothered him more than he admitted, but there was something else about them that nagged at him. Something that he had seen and tried to forget hovered in the rear of his conscious thought. An elusive fragment of information, or something that he thought should have been seen and recognised, was not coming through.

DAY TWO

Just before midnight, with the moon shining in its fullest glory, Mark gave up the struggle to sleep. He emptied most of the backpack's contents, taking only the bare necessities with him to make the return journey to the corpses. The feeling that he was missing something vital back at the site persisted so strongly that he relented to the impulse. Despite the bone-weary state of his body, despite the increased burden on his broken leg, despite the relative darkness which might cause him more injury, he succumbed to a natural instinct that told him to return.

The night was cool without being cold. His body would soon be warm with the exertion anyway. He tried desperately to find reasons not to entertain the ridiculous notion of going backwards, but his logic fell on deaf ears. He made his way slowly through the soft sand, descending to the firmer sand near the water. Millions of stars shone down upon the shore and the calm waters of the ocean.

At another time he would have considered it a perfect setting for a romantic assignation. The gentle susurration of the waves upon the shore almost lulled him into a walking sleep, making the distance slip away at an easy pace. He hobbled steadily until the sun revealed its first rays peeking over the horizon heralding the beginning of day three in paradise?

It should have been a paradise. He should have been waking up in a five-star hotel in Honolulu with room service, a full cordon bleu breakfast, and making love on silk sheets. He should have been walking hand in hand with the woman he once loved, on the beaches at night, sharing love and laughter.

Somewhere around the planet, many lovers were indulging in just such fantasies, making dreams a reality with happy memories to take with them through the rest of their days. Somehow he ended up with a kind of lunatic for a fiancée who developed evil tendencies instead of loving loyalty. The more he thought about the cruelty thrust upon him by the woman purportedly in love with him, the more it festered inside him until his rage would no longer be contained.

He let loose with a scream of white-hot anger, spewing invective into the morning air, unleashing the monster within. He felt so unjustly tormented by her actions that it tore his insides to shreds.

He had no idea what happened to the plane that caused him to be on the island with a broken leg, traipsing down the beach at all hours, but somehow he transferred all the blame for the incident on Louise's shoulders. As if she alone was responsible for everything that occurred after she dumped him so unceremoniously.

He felt comfortable blaming her for everything. It felt right to harbour and nurture the fantastic rage that was building within him. He savoured the intensity burning inside like he would a fine twenty-year-old cognac coursing through his system. He allowed the feeling to mature into a state of alarming detestation toward Louise, the cause of all the hardships he suffered.

Deep down he knew it was wrong to do so, but he didn't care, didn't listen to the guy on his shoulder for once. He was done being the good guy, done doing the honourable thing, done falling on his sword for the sake of harmony.

The insensate state he had achieved while raging at Louise had eaten away at the time it took to reach the site he dreaded seeing again. All manner of animal life had been feasting on the remains, making Mark as ill as he was before. Though he managed to keep down his meal of potato chips eaten earlier, he still felt wretched.

He chased away as much of the fauna as possible while taking in the gruesome scene, observing details in depth. In the early morning light, it all appeared quite differently compared to his previous foray. He manoeuvred himself to the opposite side, the same way he had arrived on the scene the first time. He walked about the scene with as much detachment as his mind allowed while he tried to capture the ghostly thought haunting his subconscious.

His building rage had obliterated the memory process, so he started at the beginning, going through the items of use he found, mimicking the movements among the macabre debris. He felt overwhelming guilt at not being able to bury their remains. The task was beyond his current capabilities, and he feared the effort would exhaust him to the point of near-death. He wasn't thinking straight when he first came upon the bodies.

He had thought it would be best for identification purposes if they were left uninterred, however, the opposite was probably true. Burying them in a shallow grave would possibly preserve their bodies far better than left unprotected from the elements and creatures of the island. But he could not give in to the impulse. They were destined to remain where they lay.

The mysterious answer to his niggling instinct continued to elude him as he gazed upon the last victim he had come across. It was an older lady with a floral dress, a mass of grey hair flung out from her head on the sand. The lower half of her body, minus one leg, and a foot missing from the other lay in the water being nibbled by small fish and crabs.

He sincerely regretted having returned to the site. He could not figure out what bothered him. He was no closer than when he set off on the fool's errand. He began walking back mumbling to himself that he wished he had found something more useful to his situation like fishing line or a lighter.

A lighter…matches…? Something about that train of thought. He was disappointed at not having found anything like a lighter. No, not a lighter. His actual thought process had said he was disappointed at not having found a way to start a fire! He stopped walking. Looked back. He walked back to the old lady.

Something about the old lady was not the same. Then he noticed the chain around her neck and knew what it was.

The tide had moved her hair. He fished around under her grey tresses until he found the object. He had noticed her reading glasses before and scoffed at the thickness of the lenses. He realised what an idiot he had been. The lenses were the item that tickled his antenna - another way to make a fire of course.

Mark berated himself severely for not recognising it sooner. It would have saved him an awful lot of exertion. He only then realised how red-raw he was under the arms from the friction of the crutches. He would have to spend more time at the temporary battleground in order to cut away some of the foam from the seats to cushion the armrests of his crutches.

While doing so he managed to discover two more bottles of plain water beneath one of the seats. He tied the foam around the armrests with some material he cut away from some clothing. He didn't want to think about whom the clothing belonged to. He worked for about five more minutes before being satisfied with the result.

Feeling much better about the crutches despite his underarms remaining sore, he set off once more. Basically, he hoped to explore the entire island from the beach with a view to finding a suitably sheltered area from which to base his operations. He was not overly optimistic about a rapid rescue. He remembered reading about the disappearance of a Malaysian plane that they didn't find for months. It was big news in all the media. Plan for the worst had always been his motto, and he saw no reason to change that anytime soon.

He fully believed in Murphy's Law governing all things with a merciless acuity. It may be hours, days, weeks, months, or never until help arrived, so he needed to act under the premise that if bad things were possible, they would happen.

Mark didn't lose time trying to analyse the questions surrounding the crash. Why he ended up on the beach, why he survived when obviously so many hadn't. Luck of the draw, fate, Murphy? Who knew? The fact that the pilot had flown to a lower altitude to avoid the worst of the storm would have assisted greatly he felt. He had no expertise when it came to deducing facts about the crash or where the seats landed, tides etc., so he accepted the status quo readily.

His leg still hurt like a mother but he believed he could bear it without resorting to the few remaining painkillers. Not that he wanted to be a martyr or anything noble like that, he just figured worse may be yet to come and he needed to be prepared. Hoarding a few pain killers now might save his sanity or life at a later date. He could not simply go down the road to fetch more if they ran out, so they were a precious commodity to be used sparingly.

He knew he also had to ration his water intake. He didn't know whether this island or atoll had any natural springs, creeks, or pools of freshwater despite the presence of animal life, so the few bottles he had may well be the only water available. He looked forward to the little bottle of Vodka he found. He thought he might partake of it before too long.

The sun ascended with a tropical certainty that blitzed the moisture from the pores if exposed too long. Mark opted to wait out the heat of the day in the shade provided by the foliage of the bushes beyond the dunes. If he rested up until late afternoon, he figured he would regain his forward position by evening. His leg desperately required resting as well.

The throbbing was becoming almost unbearable. It seemed to be producing some heat that could indicate an infection. Mark hoped it was not the case. Antibiotics to fight an infection would not be available to him and he had no idea what might be a suitable substitute from the natural flora around him. He didn't know his tree roots or fungi from a bowl of Fruit Loops.

Mark believed he could use logic to sort through most of his circumstances, guess at others, but he knew his knowledge of botany and marine life was somewhere between limited and non-existent. For instance; he knew there was a poisonous shell out there somewhere, but he wouldn't be able to identify the name or the appearance of that shell in a pink fit.

He knew what mushrooms looked like, but could not tell one from the other. Digging for roots may reveal a wild yam, however, he had no idea what was safe to eat as far as yams went. Pitiful really, he thought to himself. *Oh shit*, he was thinking to himself. He would be talking to rocks or something soon. It would do no good to start talking to himself or inanimate objects and certainly not anthropomorphising inanimate objects to give them semi-human qualities. That would be a sure sign he was losing it. He would leave that to Mr Tom Hanks on the Hollywood screen. No Wilsons! Note to self, no bloody Wilsons!

He wouldn't mind finding a girl Friday or similar, though, how he would manage to win her affections with a broken leg he could not imagine. He remembered seeing an old movie called 'Blue Lagoon' with a couple of young children who eventually became lovers. Hmmm, making love in paradise while dining on lobster tails. Nice thoughts to send him into his midday nap.

DAY THREE

Mark woke in the afternoon with a raging hard-on which he assumed was a good thing. His condition could not be that severe if his one-eyed snake was revelling in images of the afternoon's dreams. His leg didn't radiate the same amount of heat from prior, and while the bruising looked ugly and threatening, the swelling was no worse.

All in all, he figured he was doing okay considering his plight. After a mouthful of water and a couple of potato chips, he hobbled down to the water's edge. It was still very warm in the sun, so he decided to give himself a wash. He had to cut away his shorts and underwear to get naked. No way was he going to take the splint off. He would cut up a dress he found to make a sarong style garment. He needed the freedom it afforded him, to remain as hygienically clean as possible.

Using sand, he massaged the grit into his skin to remove the grime and the distaste of touching corpses. It felt refreshing sitting in the shallows with the waves gently washing over him. He thought that the saltwater would help him as well. It would certainly help the countless abrasions he had discovered after removing his clothing.

He couldn't help but think of his dreams again as he sat there naked. True to form, his body reacted in the appropriate manner for such thoughts. He toyed with the idea of relieving himself, looking about surreptitiously.

Thinking about it was all he had time for when he heard the distinctive sound of an engine in the distance. He got to his feet as quickly as he could, searching around frantically for a way to attract the plane should they come close enough. He hobbled up the beach for a pace or two and began to scratch lines in the wet sand with his crutch. It was hard going to keep the lines straight and in any sort of order hobbling around on one leg, using one stick as a crutch and the other as a writing implement.

Eventually, he finished with a half-way decent rendition of an SOS emblazoned across the beach in the largest letters he could manage. He realised too late that he had not heard the plane come any closer than when he first heard it. The sun was slowly sinking beyond the horizon. They would not have seen the sign in the waning light anyway. Maximum energy expenditure for zero results was not efficient. He needed a signal fire. Nothing else would work even one-tenth as well.

With his hard-on well and truly as deflated as his spirits, Mark washed away the sand he had spread all over his body during his mad scramble. Without donning his sarong or shirt, he walked away disconsolately in the direction of his furthest foray.

He didn't honestly believe he would be rescued quickly, but he hoped it might be a possibility. Failure to attract the plane weighed heavily on his mind. He should have been concentrating on getting a signal fire started instead of thinking with his dick. Hadn't his dick already gotten him into enough trouble? Actually, it hadn't been his dick at all that caused the trouble. Damn her to hell and back! That train of thought led right back to the internal rage that fermented quickly into a maelstrom of fiery expletives by the time he returned.

Though his leg throbbed and his stomach growled, Mark decided he could do nothing more that evening. He would search for a base camp and water source the following day. He had enough water to keep himself hydrated for a few days despite the soaring temperatures, but he knew he would need more eventually. Rescues like the ones he'd read about could be weeks away while they searched an enormous area along the flight path.

It all depended on if and when a mayday had been sent, and how long the plane remained in the air after the accident, terror incident, or whatever it was. Most importantly, it depended on how far from the gazetted flight path the plane deviated around the storm and on its way down.

Mark swallowed the disappointment of the day by once more berating himself for not thinking of making a fire while the sun was overhead the moment he had found the old lady's glasses. Had the fire been going when he heard the plane's engines he may well be on board a rescue-chopper by now.

He wondered how many people had survived the crash, and where they might be. Who made the footprints leading away from his position? Did the plane break up over several kilometres? What were the depths of the ocean around the area? Too deep to find the fuselage? Did any of the fuselage end up on the island or another island? So many questions. He didn't know if he had the right idea to explore the island, it just made sense to him somehow.

He would have to be more pragmatic about his plans with definite short term and long term goals. Making sure his leg healed reasonably would be his first priority. Mark didn't fancy the thought of gangrene, or amputation if left untreated. He doubted his ability to survive under those conditions. He knew he didn't have the intestinal fortitude to hack off a limb no matter how desperately he required it. That was the stuff of heroes whether factual or fantasy.

Mark was no hero, just a nerdy low-life lawyer, as he'd overheard someone describing him one day. Nobody loves a lawyer. We are all bloodsucking money grabbers to most. They had no idea of the amount of effort it took to become a lawyer, to pass the exams. The amount of information a student had to commit to memory, or scour through, to find the appropriate precedent to save some scumbag from going to jail, was enormous.

His next order of priority was to locate a suitable base camp. It would have to be off the beach, beyond the high watermark. There would be very little point in gathering firewood for a signal fire only to have it washed away with the first full tide. He would need some shade from the prevailing elements; heat during the day, chills from the evening breezes and storms when they arrived. The signal fire had to be ready to go at a second's notice with plenty of green foliage at hand to throw on the fire once it got started properly. It was the smoke that would attract a rescue.

Mark didn't know whether to explore the island thoroughly first or stay put once he found a site. He would have to play that one by ear. It was impossible to see beyond the thick vegetation in the interior to estimate how large the island may be. With his limited capacity, he was unable to navigate through the island. Whether he found a source for water or managed to circumnavigate the island first, was anybody's guess.

He felt a duty to seek out other survivors as unlikely as that scenario seemed to him. He had to keep a small fire going at all times in order to set flame to the signal fire. He would not be able to sit down with a magnifying lens at the sound of an approaching plane. There would simply be insufficient time. Mark would not be able to venture far from his base camp once he established a permanent fire.

Water, food, shelter - the basic necessities of life which everyone took for granted during their banal, humdrum lives - Mark included. How wrapped up in the everyday we become, with the traffic snarls, house payments, making ends meet and social obligations? An experience like being marooned demonstrates clearly the way we lose ourselves in our own expectations and those of others, instead of concentrating on getting the basics right.

Harmony with one's self and the relationships we form with others should be the first priority, but so seldom is, when we get trapped in the everyday minutiae of life in the city. Mark was thinking about changing his career as if that was really imperative. Changing jobs would make him happier, he thought mistakenly.

How petty it all becomes when faced with a life and death situation. Priorities? So much for the job, and the marriage to be, and all the rest. It all fades into insignificance in the face of a larger than life crisis. Fatality is final, funnily enough. Survival is by far the strongest of human instincts despite all our efforts to evade it, camouflage it, or ignore it altogether. Faced with survival, everything else runs at the rear of the pack.

The night sky shone brilliantly with stars. The moon was trying hard to hide behind a bank of a cloud. The first sign of a…fuck! There weren't a heap of stars shining like the previous evening. There was only half that amount because the rest was hidden behind a mass of dark clouds gathering for a torrential downpour.

He had not thought to put up a shelter or anything to safeguard against a possible storm. From his backpack, Mark grabbed a windcheater of semi-waterproof material, which he had gathered from among the washed-up clothes. He worked quickly to remove his sarong and T-shirt which he stuffed in the pack. He bound the pack into the windcheater as best he could to have some dry clothes to change into afterwards. Downing the vodka from the small bottle, he placed it and the empty water bottles alongside it, pushed upright into the sand. With caps removed, Mark intended to catch as much rainwater as possible in the little vessels.

His mind worked furiously to think of everything he could do to prepare himself. The bushes were too low to attract lightning and offered no danger of falling limbs. He would be cold for sure but hoped the backpack would remain relatively dry within the windcheater wrapping.

All that was left, was to wait out the storm. No sooner had the thought entered his mind when an ear-splitting crack of thunder rent the night asunder. Lightning followed which set the night sky ablaze with electricity. The ozone aroma filled Mark's nostrils as the night erupted into a maelstrom. The wind came from nowhere, suddenly battering his position with a force he barely believed possible.

It howled about him in a swirling intensity reminiscent of a cyclone he had been through as a child in North Queensland. Nothing had ever frightened him worse than that wind, which had subsided to an eerie stillness when the eye passed over their town.

Horizontal rain with sand in the mix lashed at his exposed skin like a sandblaster. He wouldn't be needing a body scrub for a long time. The wind and rain continued to swirl about him for what seemed like hours on end, when in fact, the storm had lasted a relatively short period. Mark shivered from head to toe in the gale-force winds persisting even after the rain, thunder and lightning diminished. In time, the wind began to die down, bringing welcome relief to Mark's frazzled nerves.

He reached into his backpack for the dry clothes, including the small blanket he had stuffed in there moments before the onslaught. He smiled at his perspicacity in doing so. Having the wherewithal to outthink Mother Nature brought a smile to his lips, the first one since his ordeal began. He used the windcheater on the wet sand beneath him as he lay down to sleep.

Wrapped in dry clothes and a thin knee blanket, Mark drifted off with good thoughts and newfound confidence. As a slight breeze rose, ruffling the leaves above, Mark was soon assaulted by irritating droplets of water, turning his triumphant thoughts sour.

The early morning sun revealed another glorious day on a tropical island if Mark was in a mood to accept it. Instead, daybreak saw Mark brooding about the direction his plans should take. The common theory was, that staying put in emergency situations was optimal. Bear Grylls spouted it on almost all of his survival shows even though he hardly followed his own advice. Well, it wouldn't have been a show otherwise.

Mark hoped he would never have to resort to drinking his own urine, or anyone else's for that matter. He didn't welcome the idea of eating raw insects either. He would try to find crabs and the like in the very near future if rescue was not forthcoming. His potato chips were gone and his hunger nagged constantly.

His empty bottles had been filled by last night's rain, giving him several litres of water along with his saved can of beer. Despite the weight of the backpack, Mark decided against leaving some behind as a back-up should he need to return. Exploring the island fully, at least the shoreline, seemed to be the most practical solution to finding a decent site at which to establish a base camp, find any survivors, and locate a more permanent water source. He could not rely indefinitely on rain to replenish his water supplies.

Another favourable reason for exploring the island was to search for any debris the storm may have washed onto the shore. Anything to make his wait more comfortable would be welcome. His leg continued to trouble him, which he supposed was to be expected after only a few days. It would be a long time before it healed properly and he hoped it would not have to be reset.

Mark continued to monitor the leg's progress carefully. He didn't think he would be able to put any weight on it for quite some time. Keeping the leg raised as he walked with the weight of the timber splints was wearying at best. Still, it could have been far worse, he imagined - a head injury or a festering open wound for instance.

Once everything was packed securely, crutches as comfortable as possible, he took off along the beach. The storm had scoured the beach clean of all his footprints, which was not a good thing in his opinion. Had a rescue vessel or plane arrived at the island closer to where he first awoke, the footprints would have led the search party directly to him.

He wondered if the aeroplane seats were still in clear view, or if the storm had swept them into the ocean. The more evidence of a crash in plain view, the easier for spotter planes to discover. The best method, though, still remained a signal fire. His hastily scribed SOS would no doubt have been erased by the storm as easily as his footprints.

His chances of stumbling across other survivors' footprints were equally poor. He would have to be extra vigilant for other signs of human existence on his travels. He sincerely hoped that he was not the sole survivor of the crash, that whomever had left the footprints leading away from his position had not perished. Would the rescue party continue to search for one MIA if all other souls were accounted for, dead or alive?

Questions like that have plagued crash victims since commercial aircraft first took passengers on board. No doubt they would continue well into the future unless perfect machines or perfect security prevailed. Mark supposed that as long as he kept asking questions he could be sure that at least his mind was functioning properly. No Wilsons in the picture yet. No Fridays either, sadly. He wished he could stop thinking about stories of castaways who were marooned for lengthy periods. At least he didn't have to worry about being eaten by native cannibals… he hoped. He hadn't heard of too many cannibal tribes in present times.

The sun beat down heavily on Mark as his pace dwindled to an uncomfortable shuffle. The humidity sapped his strength and willpower as he eked his way forward. In the distance, seagulls and other marine birds circled on the air currents above a patch of seawater signifying a shoal of baitfish or similar. Whatever it was seemed to be relatively close to shore.

He could see the birds diving from a great height, splashing down very near the shoreline. It made Mark quicken his pace a little. He hoped he might be able to take advantage of the birds and larger fish keeping the baitfish close to shore where he might catch a few in a make-shift net. Feeling sure he could improvise one with his backpack to make a scoop tied to a crutch, he limped his way as fast as possible to the choppy waters.

The patch of choppy water appeared far closer than in reality. Nearly ten minutes passed before he was close enough to confirm his earlier suspicions. He had his father to thank for his fishing knowledge, which allowed him to assess such possibilities from a distance.

When he was close enough he emptied the contents of the pack onto the sand. He tied the pack to the end of one of his crutches. He would not be able to handle anything longer or go out too deep anyway. The birds were continually diving into the centre of the shoal where a school of large predatory fish kept them from escaping to the open ocean. Small baitfish were jumping everywhere including onto shore where birds and crabs were quick to pounce. Pelicans floated above the shoal scooping up bucketsful of squirming fish in their massive beaks. Mark attempted to do the same thing by dipping his backpack into the water a metre from the edge. He was ecstatic as the bag, brimming with fish, surfaced at the end of his crutch.

Seconds after the bag reached the surface it was tugged back under. Mark only realised then, too late, that the predatory fish keeping the baitfish penned up against the shore, were sharks. Dozens of large sharks roiling in a feeding frenzy among the shoal. The water was boiling with the activity of all the animals in the throes of a feeding ecstasy. Mark's bag disappeared with one of the largest sharks he had ever seen at close quarters.

He didn't bother to contest the shark or challenge him for the right to his portion of the spoils, as Mark was too close to being swept up by another incoming marauder on the flanks of the first. He backed out of the water as quickly as possible with only one crutch, grateful to be alive. He could not believe his stupidity. He should have known it would be sharks keeping the shoal penned up. He had seen it often enough on nature documentaries.

In his zeal to collect some protein, he didn't take the time to look further than the shoal. Had he spied the sharks beforehand he would not have attempted such a foolish act. Not only did he miss catching any fish, but he also lost the precious backpack, or so he believed.

Before long the spectacle moved on, leaving Mark alone on the shore shaking his head in dismay, upset by his blunder. If he intended to survive his ordeal he needed to be much more mindful of nature and her power to take human life without so much as a 'by your leave'. At least his second crutch seemed to have survived the attack.

He saw the stick floating back toward the shore with the

waves. Mark shook himself out of his reverie to take stock of his situation. From that moment on he settled on a new determination to avoid silly mistakes that could cost him his life. He would have to use the one thing he knew he had that worked well, the one thing he knew he could rely on every day of his life; his brain. He had to think his way through every problem rather than act his way through.

Being stranded on some deserted island in the middle of the ocean was no joke. There were thousands of methods nature could utilise to ensure his demise. He would not survive unless he truly followed his convictions. He had to be there when a plane flew overhead or a vessel approached the island. He had to gather his wits about him, call on every reserve of strength and willpower he possessed to ensure his presence at the end. He didn't know how long that would take.

Refusing to waste time feeling sorry for himself about his situation and the reason he found himself there, if nothing else; his brain space had to be right. Time to stop fucking about like things didn't matter, like everything was fine and that it was only a matter of time before he was rescued. Hope for the best, plan for the worst. Only a truly tenacious resilience would prevail against the odds stacked against him.

He winced as he made his way towards the crutch that had washed up on the shore. It seemed the backpack had, in fact, survived the attack, albeit somewhat aerated. He scooped his meagre possessions back into the bag to embark on his quest of discovery once more.

He smiled as he hobbled onward, relieved to be alive after his close encounter. It was the closest he ever wanted to get to shark. If the shark had taken a bite of him it would have been all over red rover. No way could he have survived. He needed to be on his game. He would not be able to forecast all dangers he faced or be totally prepared for every ordeal, but he could have his brain thinking everything through like he was in a university exam or a courtroom. He walked as far as his body would allow before seeking shelter beyond the dunes for the evening.

DAY FOUR

Mark was so hungry he thought he could eat the clothing in his backpack. He had only eaten a lousy pack of potato chips in the four days since the crash. At least, he thought it was four days. He wasn't sure how long he had been strapped to his seat before he came to.

At first, he thought it might be the same day of the flight, but it didn't feel right. Mark believed he had missed a day in between. Maybe the headache he woke with was not caused by the position in which he found himself? Maybe he hit his head hard enough to knock him out? He found no evidence of a lump when he examined his head, so he wasn't sure. At any rate, he knew of at least four full days he spent on the island, with a possible fifth in which he had not eaten more than a mouthful or two.

He had to find some protein to keep up his strength. He would ponder the question as he walked. Laying up in the dunes beneath the bushes would not fill his belly or answer his questions.

He drank a little of his precious water before heading off. He could find no way into the interior of the island because of the dense foliage which would catch on every bit of clothing he wore. It would probably trip him up so often that his leg would need re-splinting and he could not face that procedure again. Walking on the harder sand at the water's edge seemed the only wise move.

He wished he had found a pair of sunglasses to combat the interminable glare. He wore the straw sunhat he found, but still, the glare nearly blinded him during the day, especially when the glare bounced off the sand and the water, hitting him from all directions.

He applied sun lotion liberally and often throughout the day to ward off sunburn. He didn't need the hassle or danger that burns would bring if he neglected his duties in that regard.

Around midday, with the sun directly overhead causing steam

to rise from the water-soaked sand, Mark felt he could go no further. He had found nothing to eat and knew his energy was waning fast. He would have to take a siesta during the hotter hours of the day if he wanted to avoid a heat stroke.

He'd seen Franky suffer a heat stroke on one of their camping trips when they had fallen asleep in the hot canvas tent. Frank had nearly died that day. It was only Mark's quick thinking of plunging him into the river that saved his life, according to the doctor. A fat lot of good that did when his brother ended up dying only a few years later anyway. Mark staggered up the beach to find a shady place to rest.

He had to set the alarm clock in his head to wake him in a couple of hours. He didn't want to lay up until the late afternoon. He thought he may have seen something in the distance. It was hard to be sure when he had to look through the shimmering heat waves hovering above the sand. Exhausted, famished, and in pain, with his leg cramping severely from having to keep it raised, he fell asleep in minutes.

Mark awoke to bird sound within the foliage further inland. He wondered if maybe there were nesting birds in there with eggs he may be able to steal. Eggs would certainly provide some much-needed nutrients. If he crept up carefully enough and if the birds had little contact with humans, without that ingrained fear, perhaps he could catch a bird or two as well?

The thought of a bird roasting over hot coals made his mouth water. The sand was extremely soft as far as he could see. He assumed that there would have to be solid earth eventually for low trees to be able to grow. He was unable to see more than a metre or two into the foliage as the contrast between sunlight and shadow was too acute.

Mark would have to crawl his way through if he decided to make the effort. He would not be able to stand or walk with his crutches. He could crawl with one crutch strapped to his back as long as he monitored every centimetre along the way. Mark could not afford to further injure his broken leg, but by the same token, if he didn't find food soon, his leg would be the least of his problems.

He stuffed a few items into his pockets that he thought might come in handy before edging his way through the leaf-strewn undergrowth. The temperature dropped discernibly once he was fully ensconced beneath the shady canopy, more so than under the meagre cover where he'd slept moments ago. Mark allowed his eyes to adjust to the shadowy realm before he proceeded. He was able to hear the raucous cry of many birds, possibly migratory terns, several metres further in.

With any luck, he would find some eggs and perhaps catch a bird worth eating. Mark assumed that he was on an atoll rather than an island. There were no hills or mountains, just dense foliage no more the three metres tall as far as he could tell.

He racked his brain to think of the geography between Melbourne and Hawaii. He deduced that he had to be further out than the Coral Sea which incorporated the Solomon Islands and bordering regions. That would put him…where? The Pacific? Hawaii was an American island which was in the Pacific Ocean. So he must have ended up somewhere in the Pacific he surmised.

If his memory served him correctly, the Marshall Islands were somewhere along the route. He knew from documentaries that the Marshall Islands contained many small atolls and larger islands. Or he may be nowhere near them at all. Guessing would do no good, or help his situation in the slightest, so he crawled on. He had to concentrate as he neared the bird sounds.

The moment he reached the nesting area all hell broke loose. A deafening cacophony of sound accompanied the outraged birds as they flew at Mark from all angles, with sharp beaks pecking, talons scratching and wings beating at him. He saw nothing but a wall of feathers advancing on him in waves of fiercely enraged birds. He could no sooner see a nest than raid it amid the barrage of abuse, so he took the wisest, though not the bravest course of action available to him. He retreated.

His choices were extremely limited considering he had very little protection against the sharp talons and beaks. He had dozens of cuts and abrasions all over him as a result of the foray. Not to mention a severe twinge in his leg as he twisted about in the cramped underbrush. He felt rather foolish and inadequate when he emerged into the sunshine.

Obviously, he could only attempt that again if he was better protected with more clothing and properly mobile. For the first time on the island, he was glad no one was around to witness his embarrassment.

"Sure Mark, just crawl in there and grab a few eggs from the stupid birds. They won't mind. Not like they care about their young, is it? Fuck me dead! Idiot!"

Mark gathered his possessions into the backpack and took off down the beach mumbling in pure disgust at his piss-poor efforts. He kept his head down to avoid as much of the glare as possible. The afternoon sun continued to radiate its heat mercilessly upon the hapless form trudging his way along the infinite shore.

Mark endeavoured to catch a few ghost crabs when they appeared, but they were too fast for him on crutches. His lack of mobility affected every plan he conceived, every thought of food gathering. He had to find another able-bodied survivor to accomplish the tasks required of survival.

If a movie was ever made of his misadventures it would be a bloody comedy. He would have everyone in Australia laughing at his pathetic attempt to gather a few fucking eggs, chasing ghost crabs, or his futile effort to catch baitfish.

Dumped by his fiancée, dumped by a plane onto a fucked-up island, dumped on by nature in the form of torrential rain, and dumped on, figuratively and literally, by a bunch of fucking birds! Fuck, he felt about as low as it was possible to feel trudging his way along the beach.

While walking onward, in the distance, he noticed strange tracks running up and down the beach. His only thoughts were that they were turtle tracks leading up from the water during the night to the top of the beach where they laid eggs, returning to the waterline in the morning. Once he pictured that scene in his mind, the tracks made perfect sense to him. Probably green turtles he thought. Not large enough to be the leatherbacks.

He thought he was rather smart knowing shit like that from all the David Attenborough documentaries he had seen. A fat lot of good it did him though, knowing shit like that. It didn't help him collect eggs from some stupid birds, or catch a few baitfish! Bloody idiot! All Mark had to do was collect the few baitfish that flopped up on the shore instead of getting greedy. He could have made a fish soup from them.

Fucking Louise! Everything bad occurring to Mark seemed to conjure up the image of Louise in his mind. Once again he allowed his fury to fester like a rotten potato in the hollow of his guts. The pure emotion burbled and bubbled within him like a witch's boiling cauldron. He savoured the ill-feeling like it was an elixir of life. He thrived on the tumultuous rage giving strength to his beleaguered limbs and his starved intellect. So disturbed was the man by the increasing tide of angst taking over him, that he failed to understand the import of his observations. Had he been thinking clearly, he may have understood that nutrition was at hand in the fresh turtle eggs laying just under the soft sand waiting to be uncovered.

Dubious to the windfall within his reach, he continued his halting gait, allowing the venomous thoughts to overtake his senses. Before long he realised he had been shouting obscenities to the wind at the top of his lungs. His hatred for Louise had built to such levels that, were she present, he could easily have choked the life out of her. He didn't think he had ever hated anyone so much in his life.

The fury gave him succour and the distraction he needed to continue along the beach despite the aching weariness he felt deep down in his bones. It gave him the fortitude to stumble along regardless of the interminable distance. The atoll seemed to go on forever.

The mirage he saw cleared away to reveal a rocky point at the head of a wide bay. 'Blue Lagoon' sprang to mind immediately upon seeing the idyllic, natural, deep water haven protected from the high seas by a coral reef. The waters of the lagoon were like a millpond with nary a ripple on the surface. In the clear waters reflected off the white coral sands, he saw a myriad of marine life in shoals of hundreds and thousands swaying to and fro in the gentle current. A few coral outcrops could be seen dotting the waters of the bay - what he would refer to as 'bombies' when he and his dad were out fishing along the Queensland coast near Cairns.

On the inner side of the bay along the top shoreline, he spied coconut palms bulging with life-sustaining fruit. Food and water combined if he could find a way to break into the fallen coconuts surrounding the trees. He believed a barnacle or oyster encrusted rock would solve that problem. Once established, it would even be possible to transport such a rock to the campsite. On the point where he stood were large rocks with crabs flitting about quietly munching on minuscule tidbits. Large oysters adorned the rocks at the low watermark.

Mark believed for the first time since opening his eyes on the atoll, that he might survive after all. He managed to find an ideal place from which to base his operations, to establish a signal fire and build a basic shelter. Nourishment existed here in abundance and when his water ran out he knew he could rely on coconut milk for survival if he failed to find any other natural water source. Coconut milk and oysters contained enough Vitamin C to prevent Scurvy he remembered from his extensive reading.

Were he not marooned with a broken leg and half-starved out of his mind, he might think he had landed in paradise. It was truly a remarkable sight to behold. He began to wipe the tears that flowed freely from his eyes. His decision to risk his strength to explore the island had paid off. He didn't feel like the comic relief from Gilligan's Island anymore. He felt more like the professor, bursting with pride for making the right call. Barring unforeseen calamities he fervently believed he could wait out the time for rescue in this bay. He need not venture any further unless he felt better and deemed it necessary.

He managed to bust open a few oysters with a hand-sized rock he found among the large boulders. He downed them with relish despite never having acquired the taste for the things at seafood restaurants. Today, they were the most heavenly dish he had ever tasted.

They were extremely large oysters and his stomach had shrunk considerably, so Mark was unable to down as many as he believed he could. He did harvest a few more which he kept in the remains of each shell topped up with seawater to augment his meal for the evening. He felt sure he would be able to get at a coconut or two before nightfall. He also wanted to get to the centre of the bay as soon as possible in order to start a fire.

He wanted desperately to be warm at night for once and have a fire going to attract possible survivors or rescuers. He was infused with good cheer as he made his way towards the centre of the bay. Once there, it was an easy decision to make camp on a raised clearing at the top of the beach. This position afforded Mark a full view of the entire bay before him. He would make a shelter of sorts the following day.

He grabbed the thick glasses from his backpack after he gathered some dry leaves and such with which to make a fire. He hoped there was enough heat left in the waning sun to start a flame. Within moments the brittle leaves caught, onto which Mark placed small dry twigs, then larger branches until he had a steady fire going. He had sufficient quantities of dry driftwood around him to keep a fire going for months, as well as enough to have a separate, large signal fire ready should he hear a plane. Mark smiled as he warmed himself by the fire despite the temperature being far too hot to require one. He celebrated with the hot beer and was soon tipsy from the effect. Without realising it, he was soon sound asleep, huddled by the fire.

DAY SIXTY

Mark chalked up his second month on the island by cutting another notch into his date stick. Sixty notches adorned the well-used stick that had been one of his crutches. He used both crutches far less after gradually placing more weight on his knitting leg. He believed he might soon be able to remove the splint completely, though he was not confident enough to attempt it just yet.

He had removed and retied the splint several times over the past month but was not one hundred per cent assured that the bones had knit entirely. He was able to get about with one crutch at a fair pace if he pushed himself. He judged his speed by being able to catch ghost crabs.

He stretched as he rose from his mat of plaited palm leaves tied to a raised bed frame of saplings unearthed from the inland scrub and stripped of all foliage and extraneous branches. He rubbed his fully bearded chin as he gazed out beyond the bay and upward to the sky for perhaps the millionth time. It was the same every day. No sign of any rescue or search plane.

His great mound of a signal fire lay dormant some twenty metres away on a cleared patch of sand well above the high-water mark. Below his raised position, on the beach, the large S.O.S. sign made from driftwood tree trunks and draped with dark seaweed to make the letters contrast with the white sand remained in place despite fierce storms lashing the island for more than a week. The sun finally appeared yesterday and he was able to light a fire again the previous evening.

Mark had given up most hope of being found after so long. He figured the authorities had searched for as long as they were able, found as many alive or dead as they could and the search had been finalised. His hope now rested with attracting a passing ship. He hoped that if a person on board a passing vessel saw a large fire on a supposedly deserted atoll they might investigate…or not.

If Mark were on board such a vessel he would figure the fire was started by a lightning strike, which had actually happened several times that he knew of. He was quite despondent and somewhat depressed, but not languishing in self-pity any longer. He was neither optimistic nor pessimistic about his situation. He accepted the status-quo without remonstration or regret. 'It is what it is' he kept repeating to himself.

His daily routine was unwavering in that his first priority every day was to ensure a variety of nourishment for the evening meal. Making sure firewood was sufficiently dry and well-stocked. Also keeping the S.O.S. aligned properly so it appeared as it should. Washing and exercising his leg ready for the rehabilitation it would require became paramount. His muscles had atrophied extensively since the break. It would involve extensive attention to regain the full use of the leg once the splints were removed. He wrapped his sarong around him for the walk down to the water.

He would wash thoroughly, morning and evening, to keep monitoring all parts of his body. Insect bites had become a major problem and ignoring raised blemishes would result in painful boils. He needed to clean his entire body with sand to wash away all the impurities associated with the insect bites and other mild cuts and abrasions sustained while attending to his daily duties.

Although Mark had wandered the length and breadth of his bay, he had not ventured any further during the time he had been there. Once his splint was removed and his leg was able to cope, he would explore, always just far enough to be able to return to his bay of an evening. He planned to gradually build signal fires as far along the beach as necessary in order to explore further but had to satisfy himself with being a homebody for the time being.

"Home, shit! I'm starting to think of this fucking bay as home already. I have a bed with a type of roof overhead and I think of this as home? What the fuck is wrong with me? No one to share in the monotony. Nothing else to do but play with me dick after everything is done for the day. Never thought I would be such a wanker. Flogging the log, slapping the salami and every other fucking thing you want to call it, but basically, it is all the same; wanking. Mark Streeton is a wanker. In more ways than one, my friend, in more ways than one."

Mark had been talking out loud to himself more and more as the weeks passed. He knew it was not a good sign, but he was damned if he knew how to stop himself. He didn't understand whether it added or detracted from his sanity. He just knew that he needed to talk every now and then or he felt he would just curl up into a ball and not move again.

So he just spoke to himself or the island in general when the mood took him. Generally, the island didn't speak back.

"Two months, you fucker. Two months you've had me here and no one is coming near you. Are you that much of a fucked-up island that no one visits you other than a few bastard birds with sharp beaks, or bloody turtles? What's wrong with you? Dress yourself up a bit, look a bit more respectable and you might attract a few more visitors to your shore, you slag. You're ordinary, you hear me? Fucking ordinary, plain, and unattractive. No wonder I can't get rescued - nobody likes you. You chase them all away with your looks before anyone has a chance to taste your other delights, like mosquitos, and lack of fucking water! Lucky I keep the old coconut shells to catch the rainwater, you old bitch! Otherwise, I would be dead, wouldn't I? Then you would swallow me up whole wouldn't you, tart? Another juicy human to add to your cache of corpses. Well, you're not getting me, you whore. Do you hear me? Find someone else to fertilise your shores bitch, it won't be me."

Mark Streeton had often wondered how his memorial service had gone over, how many people other than his mum and dad had attended. Did anyone at work care? Certainly not his clients, they would scramble over one another to get new representation the moment he didn't return their calls from prison or wherever else they may be holed up. His vexatious litigants would be screaming their injustice at being unrepresented to the highest courts in the land, in the desperate hope of having their convictions quashed.

Nothing like a missing lawyer to stir up the pot among the trash of human society. The misbegotten, mangy mongrels spewed out by the welfare system in their droves to pollute the streets and the courts. Mark was seriously burned out by his second year in, with an enormous caseload and too few innocents. His enforced holiday gave him clear insights to the world in which he himself had been imprisoned.

He had been seriously contemplating a job change because he sensed his demise far sooner than he intellectualised it. His moods were becoming more sombre the longer he was employed in the cesspool. The pond scum he represented were the stuff of recurring nightmares, and their crimes caused his skin to itch.

He looked upon his clients with absolute disdain and horror as they described their crimes without hesitation as if they were proud of themselves. The pecking order among them made him sicker still. The thieves considered themselves a class above druggies and dealers. The murderers considered everyone lower, especially sex offenders; the lowest of the low being paedophiles. Sometimes he would excuse himself to rush to the toilet to vomit away everything he had heard at a session, especially when children were involved.

Mark Streeton was not overly disappointed about being dead as far as his employer was concerned. He would remain dead to them long after he returned. His days of lawyering were well and truly over. He would find something else, return to school, whatever it took to rejuvenate his persona.

He would not actively seek companionship either. His last relationship had soured his taste for relationships enough to last several lifetimes. He admitted that might be an exaggeration. Sooner or later someone may come along with whom he would like to settle down and have the standard two and a half kids.

Only time would tell on that score. He still felt exceedingly hostile toward 'the person who must not be named'. He had forsworn to avoid mentioning her name or thinking too often of her. His hatred knew no bounds when it came to the bitch and he preferred not to upset himself on such a pleasant day.

After washing himself thoroughly and discovering no new blemishes among the existing scars, he made his way to the rocky point at the head of the bay to gather more oysters or whatever else he may find amid the low tide pools that form among the rocks.

The sun was ascending the eastern sky, showing promises of searing heat and humidity for at least a few days. A tropical thunderstorm could rear up at a moment's notice in the tropics, but Mark suspected that the storms had abated for the time being. January had crept in after the Christmas he was supposed to have spent vacationing in Hawaii.

He had spent the entire new year on the atoll so far. They departed Melbourne on the twentieth of December to capture a Christmas and New Year in a tropical paradise, which Mark believed could have been served just as well in the Whitsunday Islands, without having to traipse all over the ocean.

Just another reason he felt resentment towards 'the evil woman'. They may well have been… No, that was a stupid thought to pursue. They would not have been enjoying their holiday had she listened to his objections and flown to Hamilton Island instead. No, there was still the whole, 'I'm having someone else's baby', thing, to mess the holiday up no matter where they had gone.

Yeah, his holiday was fucked no matter where they went. She had succeeded in fucking up everything. He would probably die on this bloody atoll just so she could have the satisfaction of that as well. Worse still, he wouldn't die. Her ultimate revenge would be to have him detesting her for the rest of his days stuck on the bloody atoll. Doomed to wander its beaches by himself until he was either completely insane or dead. Great choice.

What exactly defined sanity though? The ability to comprehend? If that were true it left ninety per cent of his clients under the insane category. They comprehended absolutely nothing other than their next fix or trick. They would love to get off with an insanity plea, to spend their time in a mental facility instead of maximum prison. Those imbeciles had difficulty reading the written word, let alone comprehending the consequences of their actions.

Their cognitive skills measured zero, along with their ability to feel any remorse or guilt about their crimes. They attended courses whilst in prison only to achieve enough brownie points to warrant parole in the eyes of the board. Once on parole or home detention, they would quickly revert back to their slovenly, corrupted ways.

Nine times out of ten they would offend before their parole period had abated. Half the time, even serious offenders were released from jail far too early in his view, and the view of every victim he knew. All in the name of making room in the prisons for the increasing number of offenders cluttering the courts.

Modern civilisation had not found a solution to the problem of criminals and prisons. Life sentences for murderers was an unbelievable drain on the public purse when each inmate cost the government around thirty thousand dollars per annum. Prisons were overcrowded with new facilities or upgrades swallowing up more and more of the public dollar. Only in a future when medicine was able to accurately eradicate the criminal gene, or excise the exact point in the brain that causes the abnormal criminal intent function, would the problem come close to a resolution.

Building more prisons, longer sentences, and even the death penalty were Band-Aid measures for a wound too large to cover. Increasing population in urban areas with ever-expanding classes of the 'haves' and the 'have-nots' led naturally to rampant criminality. No present-day punishments were in any way deterring the nature of the criminal.

Lower-grade inmates, using prison as their university usually graduated with honours as fully-fledged high-grade criminals ready to cause mayhem the moment they were released. The minority, the few that do react to the harsh environment of prison are simply fodder for other inmates, or the judicial system itself, that rewards the wrong type of behaviour.

A meek and mellow person that made a mistake for which he or she was truly repentant, soon got lost in the system as a person not strong enough to rise above the dross that kept them mired in their own mediocrity. There was simply no such thing as rehabilitation, and anyone foolish enough to believe in it would soon learn otherwise.

The ridiculous term 'model prisoner' was bestowed upon the best actor among the feral multitudes. Acting contrite and remorseful comes easy to the experienced inmate, adept at manipulating the system, and the intellectual psycho-babble vomited out by the administration charged with their rehabilitation, benefitted no one. Millions of taxpayer dollars wasted on ineffectual courses aimed at improving the mind and sensibilities of Neanderthals only one step removed from animals.

Mark felt like climbing to the top of the largest boulder to shout his proclamations to the world. Atop his soapbox rock, he would let the world know of its many wrongs and how it should go about fixing them. Unfortunately, he didn't have the answers either, so he didn't deign to preach his sermon today. Raving against the powers that be would not solve his predicament, or procure his daily nourishment, so he opted to utilise his eyes and hands rather than his oratory skills.

He was soon lost to the task, scraping juicy oysters off the rocks at the low water mark, catching a few small fish trapped in the shallow pools, being very careful to avoid anything of which he was unsure. Getting stung by a stonefish or bitten by sea snakes would result in certain death for him. Something he hoped to avoid for the duration of his own sentence.

He deemed his time on the atoll as a form of punishment for a wrong he had committed to someone, somewhere. His sentence for that infringement was hard labour on a tropical island in solitary confinement. His walls were the waters of the ocean that prevented his escape. He didn't have the tools with which to fashion even a rudimentary craft to convey him beyond the tranquil waters of the bay to the open ocean where he may come across a trade route or fishing vessel. Unlike regular inmates in solitary confinement given one or two hours a day of reprieve to stretch their legs outside their cells, Mark had no such luxury. The penance for his crime was the constant struggle for survival.

Every day he needed to find sufficient protein and nutrients to sustain life. Fear of his cellmates outweighed anything his counterparts had to face in their tame surroundings. If he placed a foot wrong, he could be eaten by the first shark to venture his way. In prison, three square meals were provided each day of a prisoner's sentence. Albeit a meal fit for a dog, Mark would gladly settle for that type of glorious repast compared to his coconut and seafood diet.

Given the exact same food every day, even the most exotic ingredients lose their appeal in short order. He longed for a thick, char-grilled steak dripping with fatty juices, topped with a pepper and mushroom sauce, accompanied by potatoes in their jackets served with garlic butter, honeyed carrots and minty peas.

Any kind of red meat would be a welcome addition to the strict diet of seafood and coconut. Shit, even Brussel Sprouts would be a glorious gastronomic delight in the circumstances. Mark wiped away the bit of drool that escaped his lips at the thought of meals that didn't include seawater. As he stretched his back from the labours of bending all morning, shielding his eyes from the glare, he thought for a moment that he spied a shadow back at his camp. It was a fleeting glimpse of something that was incongruent with his normal perception of the camp. There was no repeat of the movement, so he paid scant attention to it, continuing with his hunting and gathering.

Mark finished his duties among the rocky outcrop then began to make his way to the fish trap he had designed from rocks at the low watermark. It was a simple 'Y' construction nestled in against the rocks so that as the tide went out, fish would enter the open section at the top, make their way down to the end of the straight section to be met with a dead end. By the time the fish figured it had reached a dead-end, it was too late to retrace its way to the entrance as the tide had fallen too far.

In theory, it sounded just great. In practice, however, he seldom managed to catch any fish. The larger ones simply jumped over the wall into the open water, bursting through the light, plaited-leaf roof he constructed. He did manage to trap a few small fish, though, and with those, he made a mash of sorts that he roasted on a rock beside his fire. Once he secured the two tiny fish he had caught in his trap that day, dispatching them humanely with a snap of the neck, he wandered casually back.

At some point on his limping stroll toward his camp at the centre of the bay, Mark became aware of a subtle change. At first, he was unable to identify the change if, in fact, there was one. He halted his walk to take in as much detail as possible, to ascertain the factor that was making the hairs on the back of his neck stand on end. As he trawled through the image he settled on the smoke rising from the fire.

Nothing unusual about that at first glance because he always stoked up the fire and loaded it up before venturing forth each day on his hunt. Seeing smoke rising from his campsite was not surprising, but dawning on his suspicions gradually was the fact that more smoke rose from the fire than could be expected after being left alone for many hours. In fact, the fire seemed to be roaring! Mark hoped the fire had not somehow spread to other parts of the camp.

He was unable to sprint to the camp and didn't believe the effort would save anything from an out of control fire in any case, so he continued to make his way along the beach at his usual pace.

He lifted his head from time to time without witnessing anything that altered his opinion of the situation.

His calm was soon eradicated by the vision of both fires burning. His signal fire had somehow ignited causing the amount of smoke billowing across the beach and into the sky. He was dismayed by the fact that he would have to regather an enormous amount of firewood to rebuild the signal fire. It just galled him that all that original effort was wasted with no one to signal. Half-heartedly he scanned the horizon to see if perhaps he might be lucky enough to make use of the accidental signal. He saw nothing out of the ordinary.

"Hey, hey, I'm here. Hey there…Mark? Mark? Is it really you, Mark?"

Mark was temporarily paralysed by the sight of the person advancing toward him. Words were unavailable to him, as the last person in the world he wanted to see began running toward him with outstretched arms, tears streaming from her eyes, jubilation etched on her sunburnt features.

He began back peddling as fast as his body allowed before he toppled ungracefully to the sand. As she approached with pure joy suffusing her face, Mark recoiled in abject horror. He turned over to start crawling away from the advancing nightmare. Terror, anger and frustration wrestled violently atop one another for prominence among the storm of emotions assailing him as she caught up with him.

"Mark? It's okay, Mark, it's me, Louise."

"I know who the fuck you are!"

Mark turned over and sat up straight, looking into the face of his arch-enemy. The nemesis that brought down all of the catastrophes he had encountered since the ill-fated flight. He was struggling with inner demons that wanted to banish the woman from all existence with as much physical pain as possible.

He strove to prevent himself from simply launching upon her, to subdue her, carry her to the bonfire where he would cast her alive upon the roaring flames. His frenzied, crazed mind cast his eyes in the direction of the blaze. Louise, sensing his confusion at the fire, stated brazenly…

"Yes Mark, the signal fire. It was such a good idea. I made sure it was lit so that we could be rescued."

"You?"

"Yes, I lit the fire for you."

Mark was seething, barely able to keep himself from strangling the living daylights out of the moron before him. He struggled to a standing position shrugging off her proffered hand to assist. He made his way to the campsite where he found upturned coconut shells devoid of the precious water he had saved therein. The last of his food from the previous day devoured and the scraps were strewn about haphazardly.

His eyes were watering from the insensitivity shown so evidently by the intruder. She had encroached upon his sanctity, his home. The vile, evil bitch had invaded his privacy, started the signal fire, purposely, while eating his food and drinking his precious water. His blood boiled, he was incensed, enraged, infuriated beyond any measure. He turned on her.

"How dare you defile my camp, eat my food and drink my water! How dare you start my signal fire?"

"Mark, don't you want to be rescued?"

Mark lost it. He was no longer the person she once knew. He was the product of two months of stored up torture and torment all finding its way to the surface. He could contain his fury no longer, he was losing control of all his faculties as the target of his rage was finally at hand. He pushed her hard, with every ounce of his strength, sending her sprawling some two metres distant.

"You fucking imbecile! Rescue? Can you hear a plane, see a ship? It took me the better part of a week to gather all that firewood with a broken leg so that I could start a fire the moment I heard or saw signs of a search party. But no, you think that by lighting my fire, they will come! Like they are just waiting, poised to jump the second they see a sign from you! Why didn't you start your own fucking fire if you felt that way? Why did you have to come here and spoil everything, ruin my signal fire, eat my meagre rations of food and water? Why did you have to come here at all? Why? Why? WHY?"

Louise lay still, in total shock at having been brutally shoved to the sand by Mark. She instinctively placed a hand on her abdomen showing sure signs of the pregnancy. She was bewildered by the rage consuming her fiancé making him so violent. He looked as though he wanted to kill her and she felt very unsafe.

After so long by herself, she couldn't believe her good fortune at finding someone else alive, let alone that it turned out to be Mark. She admitted that she perhaps could have waited to be invited to eat and drink his food, but she was starving and thirsty, to the point where manners didn't enter her thoughts.

It still didn't explain the intensity of his anger, or the look of pure hatred evident in his eyes, the manic appearance of him. She decided that retaliation of equal anger might not be her best defence at that moment.

"Look, Mark, you're right, I shouldn't have just barged into your campsite and helped myself like that. It was rude and insensitive. I'm sorry. I have no excuse other than to say that I was on the verge of starvation and dehydration. I, I didn't think about the fire, sorry. It was the first time on the island I had seen fire and the thought of rescue just had me so excited. I have a baby to care for Mark and I can't just think of myself anymore. So if we can just go back to camp and talk about…"

"No way are you going to share my camp. You've survived this long by yourself, you can fuck off and continue to survive by yourself."

"You can't be serious, Mark? We have to work together now that I found you. We…"

'Why? You walked away from me once already. Those were your tracks in the sand, leaving me there in that bloody seat, alone, with a broken leg, weren't they? No, we don't have to work together. Anyone else in the whole wide world walking up that beach, from Jack the Ripper to Ronald McDonald, would have been welcome to sit by my fire and share my food. Not you. The one person in the history of mankind I didn't want to see again, is not welcome here. I was happy with the thought that you were dead. I am now greatly upset by the fact that I was wrong."

"Mark, what's happened to you? I don't understand why you're behaving like this."

"Then you have a very defective memory for an ex-fiancée. You have a bastard in your belly which you tell me about on the way to our holiday, then leave me to die after the bloody plane crashes."

"I don't really remember just after the crash. I remember walking, walking a long way. That's all. I, I had a big lump on my head and that may be the reason..."

"I am not listening to your lies. I don't care. I've managed without you up to now, and I imagine I will continue after you're gone."

"But, Mark, we can help each other."

'Yeah, you've been a great help so far. Two minutes here and you've cost me weeks of hard work. No, I am not glad to see you, I thought I made that perfectly clear. Let me spell it out for you. F.U.C.K. O.F.F.! I hate your guts! Leave, now!'

"Why, Mark?"

"Why? Can you really be asking me that? You dumped me, remember? Did you think I wouldn't remember that? Did you think it wouldn't make a difference, that I would welcome you with open arms despite being stabbed repeatedly in the back? Gee, Honey I am so glad I found you even though you don't love me anymore and are having a long-term affair with one of your freaky mates who gave up being queer just long enough to impregnate you. Is that how you saw it? No way, José. You wanted me out of your life and out of your life I will stay."

"Mark, please, we need each other to survive."

"Wrong! I don't need you. What I need is a caring person who doesn't want to rip my heart out and eat it for breakfast. I survived all this time with a broken leg so don't give me that bullshit. I don't need you to survive, I am doing quite well without anyone's help."

"Alright, alright, then I need help to survive. Me and the baby Mark, we need some help if we are going to make it."

"Call the bastard's father to help you. My schedule is full. I don't care about you or the bastard you're carrying. I don't care if you make it or not. In fact, I prefer if you didn't. If you stay here with me I may just make certain you don't. I'll just bury you somewhere inland afterwards. No one would be any the wiser, and believe me, I am more than capable of carrying it out. You have no idea how much hate I have for you, how many times I have pictured your rotting corpse washed up on the beach somewhere. I have visualised your death in so many ways that I've lost count. Go, get out of here. You have nothing to offer me other than your body and I would sooner cut my dick off than allow it anywhere near your stinking hole again."

Louise raised herself to her feet with as much dignity as she could muster, then dropped her head to her chest resignedly.

"By the way, do you remember my younger sister, Brianna, whom you detest so much that you would not allow her into our house?" Louise nodded uncertainly without looking up. "Well, Brianna called me to meet her, to help her celebrate her successful audition. She was still in costume from her dress rehearsal when I met her at the train station that day. Yes, she was dressed as a prostitute for her part in the play on Flinders Street, and could only get away from the rehearsal for a short time which was why I couldn't join you and June for lunch that day. She met me at Flinders Street station because I caught the train to the city instead of fighting the traffic. I never cheated on you and never would have."

Mark turned his back on Louise for what he desperately hoped would be the last time in his life. He knew deep down that it would not be the case, she would cause more problems for him, but he continued to hope none-the-less. He didn't look back as he marched resolutely to his camp.

His hauteur was not lost on Louise as she stood there open-mouthed with shock. Was it true? Could it have possibly been his sister Brianna? She always was a little tart which was part of the reason Louise disliked her so. They had fallen out from the moment they first met, when Brianna spoke openly of her brazen affairs and one-night stands.

Louise thought hard about the day she saw Mark at the train station and admitted, regretfully, that it could possibly be true. Had she thought to look closer she would have seen the distinctive birthmark so evident on Brianna's neck, looking exactly like a map of Australia.

Louise could not believe how foolish she had been not to confront Mark on her observations. She had left him no option than to see his sister in private given the way Louise felt. He was honouring her wishes by agreeing to see his sister outside their home and she had totally misread everything. Her guilt was overwhelming, her posture slumped like she didn't have the will to go on.

The tears dripped freely to the sand as she stood there in anguished torment over her abhorrent behaviour. She understood why Mark had acted with such vehemence toward her. Were the shoe on the other foot she may well have acted the same. Ashamed and alone she trundled back disconsolately in the direction of the point from which Mark had come. There was nothing behind her to assist any further in her survival, she had taken advantage of every opportunity back there where she first found herself after her long walk two months ago. She had marked off the days in her own way.

She was lucky enough to have found a rustic shelter slightly inland which she guessed to be a scientific observation post from long ago. The galvanised iron tank beside the shack had enough freshwater to sustain her for as long as she remained, and she had found enough provisions washed up on the shore from the plane wreck to keep her hunger at bay. That was until the airline food became too rancid to eat and the rainwater tank collapsed due to wood rot in the supports.

It was the reason she had to move on. When she saw tendrils of smoke above the inland trees from time to time, it buoyed her spirits into thinking survival might be possible. The thought of being near a fire excited and thrilled her so much that she made her way around the atoll very quickly. She was disappointed at first to see only the bare rudiments of a make-shift shelter when she approached the campsite. She had hoped it might be a fisherman's hut or another scientist's shack where rescue would be a very real proposition.

She was grateful for the little food and water however, and thought excitedly about lighting the bonfire after having been without any heat for so long. The little fire just didn't seem enough and the idea of attracting a rescuer was too tempting to ignore. She understood her folly of course. It wasn't a matter of 'build it and they will come'. It was a matter of waiting for signs of a search party or something and only then lighting a signal fire.

She understood that now. Louise understood a great many things now but it was all too late. What she had done to Mark was unforgivable, reprehensible, totally disrespectful and hateful. Her gross shame suffused her spirit, casting her into a bottomless pit of despair and misery. She left the bay feeling very depressed and unwanted.

Louise had to concentrate on her baby's survival which meant more to her than her own, however, the two were inextricable. If Louise didn't survive, then neither would the baby. She was very scared about still being on the atoll when the baby arrived.

She was around was two months pregnant at the time of their flight and just beginning to show, which would put the birth somewhere around June. She didn't believe she would still be marooned by then, but doubts gnawed at her. Having a baby without a hospital nearby could be perilous for a woman on her own, despite her distant ancestors doing so for centuries.

Primitive women also lost a lot of babies and their mothers during childbirth she argued. Food, water, and shelter were her highest priorities, always were, but the likelihood of obtaining all three in the near future was highly unlikely. She would have to remain near the bay where Mark lived to beg, borrow or steal whatever she needed to survive. Niceties be damned where life was at stake; she felt sure that Mark would realise that eventually. He would have to give in, allow her to stay with him.

She had no choice in the matter. Alone, she would die very soon. She had used up all her luck finding the resources close by on the other side of the atoll but held no false hopes for a repeat of her good fortune. Living off the land for her would simply be impossible.

Aiding in her dilemma would be the weight gain of pregnancy. Flapping about like a beached whale was going to seriously undermine her efforts to feed herself or build shelter and gather wood. She had no means with which to start a fire which meant the nights would get a lot colder as the months dragged on. She would wait around the point keeping a sharp lookout for when Mark left his camp to hunt at the other end of the bay, or out in the bay itself. There were certainly inherent risks involved no matter what she decided with Mark being the least of her concerns.

She didn't honestly believe he would seriously harm her. Mark was a pussycat inside, a marshmallow interior, incapable of harming women. It was one of the things that attracted her to him in the first place after many a failed relationship with dictatorial males.

Mark was very different from anyone she had ever gone out with. He acted like a loyal puppy dog until his job started getting to him and the arguments began. She never believed he would cheat on her until she saw him at the train station and thought all the wrong things and felt so hurt by his supposed betrayal. Chalk up one case of the stupids to Louise Campbell on that score. Major, major fuck-up with drastic consequences on her part. His sister! Oh, how could she not have seen that? Brianna was a very distinctive young woman, so she should have recognised her.

Louise didn't give Mark the benefit of the doubt either. She refused to see any other explanation for his secret rendezvous in the city, after informing her that he would be unavailable for a lunch with her and June. Stupid, stupid, stupid she kept repeating until exhaustion saw her curling under a bush to rest awhile. Tomorrow her plan would be implemented. To get back together with Mark by hook or by crook, anything and everything was fair game when lives were at stake. That was the mantra she silently mouthed as she drifted off.

DAY SEVENTY

Mark knew that his camp was rat-infested. He saw the signs every time he returned to camp. It wasn't that obvious at first but soon became apparent when small things were misplaced or food went missing. Interesting rats though, they seemed to be able to lift heavy pieces of wood onto the fire which burned brighter than it should each time he returned.

He had not seen any tracks leading to or from his camp which suggested a very clever rat indeed, using the soft sand at the top of the beach among the driftwood to hide its tracks. His water also continued to diminish despite his strict rationing practices. He had taken to keeping all his food stores with him whenever he ventured out of late. He stored whatever remained of his water supplies in the plastic bottles which he then secreted at a location well away from his camp. Sooner or later the Rat would be desperate enough to try another tack. He would be ready for it.

Days blended into one another as the passage of time eked by at an agonisingly slow pace. How was it that time never advanced at the same rate when he was at work? He never seemed to have sufficient time to finish his day's activities when he was a lawyer. His caseloads increased the longer he laboured to wade through the mass of briefs burdening his desk.

How quickly days went when he desired more time to properly acquaint himself with new clients, with their ever-increasing dependence on him the closer their trial dates approached. He felt constantly ravaged by the onward assault of time on his duties. He felt like Mickey Mouse in Fantasia with the never-ending brooms supplying limitless buckets of case files over his desk until he was drowning in them. He woke up often screaming from that particular nightmare. There was no reprieve from the onslaught of criminals requiring representation.

He had not had so much as one day off in the years he was with Legal Aid. His first and most important of holidays turned into the worst kind of experience he was ever likely to encounter. *So much for a holiday*, he thought. Highly overrated in his estimation considering his track record. He would be sure to limit his travels and restrict their distance in future. If he had a future where holidays were concerned, that is.

His enforced holiday may extend into eternity if he was unable to signal a passing ship. Without fully exploring the rest of the atoll he had no idea if a long-term water supply was available. His dwindling supplies would not last long without a steady influx of rain squalls to fill his bottles and coconuts. It would last even less if the Rat found his cache.

He thought of ways to trap the Rat without using his precious food or water as bait. He could always stay in camp for a few days without going out to forage? He didn't like the idea, but it may come to that. No better way of guarding his possessions than by staying close to them.

That would force the Rat to keep its distance or reveal itself. The scenario held its merits. He liked the thought of seeing the Rat begging for food or baring its teeth in a show of false ferocity. That would be amusing for a while, something to pass the time. The downside of the plan would be that he would have to play catch up to restock his food supply, which took the better part of the day to procure. The large oysters were damn difficult to remove whole from the rocks and waiting for the tide to turn kept him away until after dark at times. He would have to ponder the problem longer until a satisfactory plan revealed itself.

As he made his way to the small cluster of rocks at the opposite end of the bay, he wondered if his latest invention had proved successful. He managed to make a lobster pot of sorts with saplings and plaited coconut leaves. He used some small crabs and coconut flesh as the bait. He positioned the pot near the opening to a small grotto a few metres out, beneath the waterline.

With the tide receding to extremes lately, he hoped the pot would be accessible without having to dive for it. Placing the pot was easy enough when all he had to do was throw it out to the right position. He didn't fancy having to retrieve the pot by swimming in among the ever-present sharks. While his leg was still a hindrance with the splints weighing him down, he didn't relish his chances against the eating machines of the sea.

He spied the trap just under the water but accessible on foot. He didn't detect any movement within the pot as he drew nearer. He was saddened to think the trap had not worked. He'd seen a couple of crayfish under the water as he sat on a rock a few days ago, which gave him the thought of trapping them. He initially believed he might catch them at low tide while standing no more than waist-deep in the water, but witnessing several sharks prowling the area, he decided on making a trap instead. He would be disappointed if he failed to catch one, however, he would not give up and felt sure he would succeed in time.

To his surprise and delight, he barely managed to lift the pot out of the water with three massive crayfish thrashing about as the pot hit the air. The abundance of fresh food introduced an entirely new quandary for Mark. He baulked at cooking and eating three large prizes in one day. On the other hand, he didn't want sharks getting too familiar with them if he should keep two in the pot at the present location. He didn't want to waste a single morsel of his precious treasures. Not to sharks and not to…rats.

The answer was relatively straightforward in the end. He simply carried the pot to a pool within the rocks at a higher point which never dried up and was deep enough to maintain its cool temperature, as it was positioned in such a way that the sun hardly found its way to the pool at all. As he was at the eastern end of the bay and a certain rat suspect was located beyond the western side of the bay, he felt sure his plunder was safe.

He grasped the crusty feelers of the crayfish as he lifted it from the pot. He placed the flicking brute into his backpack before carefully placing the pot within the pool, laying rocks and branches over it to weigh it down and protect it further from the heat. He salivated as he imagined the feast he would have that evening. He silently whooped for joy, being careful not to arouse the curiosity of the Rat.

He smiled as he realised he could go ahead with plan A, as a result of his hunting skills. He would sneak out of camp just before first light the following day to retrieve another crayfish from the pot, then hightail it back to camp before daybreak to forestall any poaching. Two or more days of that should see the Rat expose itself.

As he made his way back to camp he recited a phrase over and over. 'The Rat, the Rat, the dirty little Rat. The dirty little Rat is heading for the trap. The Rat, the Rat…' Mark was definitely excited at the prospect of lying in wait for the Rat. The adrenaline coursed through his body making him shiver with delight. He stole furtive glances about him as he hugged the prize close to his chest.

Mark became more possessive each day about his spoils from the hunt and the things he had made from scratch at his camp. He would defend his possessions to the hilt against any foe, human or otherwise. Every day he was able to place more weight on his broken leg, freeing up his movements about the camp and on his hunts. He would even be able to explore the interior gradually over the coming weeks. Once he got rid of the Rat, that is. He had to make sure everything was safe before he could possibly leave it.

***

Louise didn't see Mark leave his camp the following morning for the first time since monitoring his movements. He would normally leave the camp for a wash down at the water's edge early in the morning, then wander off in the nude allowing the rising sun to dry him off. Although terribly thin from lack of suitable nourishment, he appeared a bronze Adonis to Louise as she watched him walk up the beach using a stick as a cane. His hair was growing long and his beard was quite bushy. There was a strange animal attraction about him. The aura of a self-assured man off to hunt for the day. His skin had the lustre of a healthy Polynesian native going about his daily activities. She envied him his resourcefulness in acquiring his food each day without fail.

The rudimentary bed and shelter he had erected at the campsite and his ability to administer first aid to himself impressed her. Everything a proper man should be able to do it seemed. So unlike the lawyer she knew and had grown weary of. So different to the slump-shouldered man she saw coming home each day from work with all the worries of the world weighing him down.

If Louise was not mistaken, she was beginning to fall in love with her fiancé all over again. She saw signs of the Mark whom she first met. An upstanding man among men, assured, intelligent, and strong of body and mind.

That man was resurfacing before her eyes on the beach each day. A man with purpose and determination apparent in every stride. A man of conviction and responsibility, ensuring his survival against the odds. Louise, on the other hand, had capitulated to the circumstances in which she found herself. She had not rationed her water or food while on the other side of the atoll. She had not paid attention to the failing support beneath the water tank. Mark would probably have seen to that immediately, ensuring it was strong enough to continue to hold the weight.

Louise knew she had wasted a lot of her time lying about idly waiting for a rescue instead of planning for a worst-case scenario. Her skin felt like leather as the sun continued to play havoc with it. She had lost count of the number of times her skin had burned in the harsh sunlight. Her clothes were simply rags with gaping holes in the threadbare fabric. She wished she had worn a full-length sundress instead of the short, sleeveless, floral shift that barely managed to cover her body, let alone keep the sun at bay.

Her hair was a bedraggled mess, her armpits a hideous, hairy cesspool, and her feet were severely calloused from walking on hot sand for months. When she saw her reflection in the water she hardly recognised the gaunt features staring back at her. She looked like one of those pictures she had seen of victims at Auschwitz. Her emaciated limbs were incongruent with the enlarged abdomen she gained with pregnancy. Or perhaps it was in keeping with the look, like the starving children of Ethiopia, or wherever the pictures in Africa came from.

She detested seeing the commercials of the starving children. Most times she walked away or turned the television off when the ads came on. She never donated to any charity, especially for the starving children. She always felt like taking a plane over there just to tell them to stop making the bloody children in the first place, then they wouldn't have such a huge problem. Abstinence was probably the answer if castration was out of the question. Well, okay, so that went too far, so perhaps vasectomies would suffice? Nice simple operation without the need for general anaesthetic.

Australia had its own starving black children among the Aboriginals on the missions. Every picture ever taken included the ubiquitous run of thick green snot protruding from their wide nostrils, with flies buzzing about it like it was a feast to end all feasts. Just the thought of it made her stomach revolt.

Louise groaned as the sickness came upon her again. Every day the sickness would descend upon her in waves of perpetual nausea and constant vomiting. She was unable to look at food without feeling desperately ill. Despite being stick thin, she felt bloated all day long. Her back ached intolerably while she grew weaker and weaker. It was an effort just to rise each morning to continue her vigil.

Whenever she saw Mark leave his camp, she would make a bee-line for it, keeping to the driftwood line as much as possible in order to hide her tracks. The effort was hardly worth the rewards of late with nary a scrap of food or water to be found. Not that she could keep down the food at any rate. At least he had a permanent fire going with which she could warm herself in the early hours. The nights were becoming cooler as well, though not cold by any means.

The cool of the night was exaggerated by the heat of the day Louise thought. Most days saw her hiding underneath foliage to escape the worst of the sun's damaging rays. She was a melanoma waiting to happen without any protection at all. Mark found enough sun cream to keep him going but tended to either take everything with him every day or hide it.

Whether or not he knew about her incursions into his inner sanctum, or he was just being cautious, she was unsure. Louise thought that Mark may be aware of her visits, but that he didn't seem to mind. Louise would not make the same mistakes again of eating all his food or drinking a lot of his water, but she doubted he would trust her. Her thirst raged since he took to hiding or taking his water with him. She managed to lick a few dew drops from leaves each morning but had little else to quench her insatiable thirst.

She decided to take the risk of entering Mark's camp by making her way cautiously along the beach. She surmised that Mark had left the camp at dawn, believing she had risen too late to witness his departure.

The trek along the beach grew longer each time she traipsed its dreary path. She made her way along the driftwood line while keeping her eyes peeled for the slightest movement at any point along the beach, never knowing from where Mark might appear. Once, when she thought the coast was clear he nearly caught her fully exposed on her way to his camp. He appeared suddenly from the top of the beach halfway to the point, adjusting his sarong around his waist. Luckily he didn't look her way as he made his way to the rocks at the eastern end of the bay.

She couldn't be sure what he was doing among the inland shrubbery, or how far he could manage with his leg still in a splint. She had heard the occasional bird cry from inland and assumed he was extending his hunting paths to include portions of the interior. Louise had been unable and unwilling to venture within the dense foliage during her time.

The first time she attempted it she became disoriented and fearfully lost after only a few metres in. It was surprising how dense the foliage was despite there being no evidence of soil with which to nourish the bushes and low-growing trees. She often heard grunts and squeals coming from the bushes at night. When she had the science shack to shelter in, she felt quite safe, but sleeping in the open scared her senseless each night. She often lay awake at night listening to the sounds emanating from the interior. The squeals were almost human-like, which set her imagination running rampant and her nerves on edge.

When she finally reached the camp she sighed with relief. Mark was not able to see her from his low position on the point when she sat at his campfire, but she was able to see just above the dune down the length and breadth of the beach. If she saw Mark coming her way she would simply scamper off along the top of the dune in a low crouch until she reached the western point. The trek was too difficult to traverse each day, so she kept it only as her escape route. Very little of any use lay about the camp that morning.

Louise wished she could risk a short nap on his make-shift bed, but she knew better. If Mark caught her in his camp, on his precious bed, he would make it very difficult for her. She didn't feel as though Mark would harm her more than a shove or two, it just wasn't in his nature. She was always comfortable, knowing she was safe in their relationship.

Luke, on the other hand, had taken to drinking rather heavily before she left with Mark on their trip, often threatening her with physical assault if she didn't go along with his increasingly perverse demands. She didn't believe what Mark told her about Luke being bi-sexual in the least. Although, he did like going in her rear end more often than not. She acquiesced readily enough to most of his 'special' times, as he liked to call them. They often included role-play, handcuffs and other toys. She didn't even think it odd when she jokingly started inserting those same toys into him.

Her experience of such things was limited to Luke alone. With Mark, it was always far more conventional, and she had very few long-term relationships before him. She just believed that Luke didn't mind getting a bit of what he gave out is all. She found it to be fair-minded behaviour if anything. She certainly hadn't seen any evidence of his infidelity with anyone of either sex. Not like… Well, Mark didn't either, did he?

She dredged up the memories of that day at the train station for evidence of Mark's testimony. To her shame, she realised what an absolute fool she had been. She believed she saw Brianna's birthmark in her recollections, something she should have noticed that day. Mark was telling the truth and it was all her fault that the relationship foundered from then on.

With the exception of one evening when they were both drunk, she refused to sleep with him from that fateful day. It was easy enough to avoid his advances as they were few and far between. His mind was absorbed with his work, day and night, often waking up with cold sweats in the middle of the night, or crying out in his sleep.

He was perpetually exhausted, making it easy for her to slip away to be with Luke at every opportunity. When she found out she was pregnant, everything changed. She made plans with Luke to reveal the truth in Hawaii. Luke was to meet them there so that they could hash it out together. She meant to confront Mark, with Luke's support, about his infidelity.

She was hoping to lay the groundwork for the intervention they had planned upon reaching Hawaii, but the damn plane blew up. Louise heard two distinct explosions, one being from the direction of the cockpit. The plane veered way off course without a pilot to guide it. She was in no doubt that no emergency call went out before the cockpit was obliterated by the explosion. Louise had been thrown forward in her aisle seat, she saw the gaping hole at the front of the plane. She saw many people jettisoned from the craft through that opening. Then the rest of the plane began to come apart under the immense forces. Cabin luggage and assorted debris, cargo, seats and the like splashed down all about her as the plane continued to disintegrate.

The impact of landing in the water from a great height knocked her head against something rendering her momentarily unconscious. The wind was driven from her lungs before she sank beneath the waves. It took all her strength to regain the surface. In truth, she had merely been a few feet in the water, strapped to her seat next to Mark.

She feared greatly for her life the entire time she remained in the water. Shark activity abounded near her, but thankfully, concentrated on the people who were dead or dying. She tried hard not to think of what might happen to her before she escaped her seat. Once she managed to release herself from her seat, she wasted no time in leaving the area. In all the confusion and the fear, she thought nothing of the other passengers and her partner sitting next to her. In truth, she could not recall if Mark were next to her or not.

Louise staggered about for most of the day unsure of what to do or where to go. She thought about signalling for help, even heard the occasional sound of an engine in the distance throughout the day, however, she had nothing with which to signal a plane. She was never a Brownie or a Girl Guide, so she knew nothing about starting fires without matches. She was certainly not going to start rubbing two sticks together, that's for sure.

It was nearly nightfall when she stumbled into an inlet with signs of human habitation. She spied a shelter of sorts nestled in among the shrubs. She almost collapsed with exhaustion into the rudimentary abode where she slept fitfully until the heat woke her the following day. By that time her throat felt parched and her stomach grumbled its annoyance at her.

Louise found nothing of consequence around her to assist her plight until she spied a tap coming through the wall at the height of what may have once been a kitchen benchtop. She opened the tap gingerly, unsure of what to expect after discovering that it was connected to a rainwater tank on the other side of the wall. It smelled okay, meaning it was not befouled by dead animal matter as far as she could tell. A filter of sorts appeared to be operational between the tank and the outlet in the shack. She tasted the water with apprehension, fearful of harmful bacteria. She didn't want to end up dying through severe gastroenteritis or whatever the hell else someone could get from contaminated water. It tasted so good that she threw caution to the wind and simply gulped down the water until she felt her thirst assuaged.

There was sufficient water in the tank according to her investigations to last her as long as necessary. Louise wandered outside to explore the immediate area to find food if possible. It was not long before she found several sealed polystyrene containers filled to the brim with fully wrapped airline food - packages of sandwiches, cake and biscuits.

Louise could not believe her good fortune. In the containers, there was enough food to see her through to the rescue that she believed would come soon. She shouted for sheer joy. She was physically unscathed by the crash, unmolested by sharks during her time in the water, had found food, drinking water and shelter without having to overly exert herself. Louise imagined she had the whole survival thing down pat.

By the time the storms came two months later to wipe out her water supply in one fell swoop, the remains of her food supply had spoiled and she became far less cocksure of herself. When thirst and hunger threatened to overwhelm her and with the sun causing major problems for her skin, she had advanced her explorations only a few kilometres along the beach.

Spurred on by the sight of a few wisps of smoke above the tree line of the interior, she eventually made her way to Mark's bay where she made a complete shit of herself. Who could blame Mark for being angry with her? She had no right to invade his campsite, helping herself to his limited supply of food without permission.

Then she undid all his hard work by setting light to his signal fire. She couldn't have done worse if she'd tried. She didn't blame Mark for being more than a little upset. He had every right to be angry with her, and she deserved the harsh treatment of being shoved.

A missile landed fair-square on Louise's chin, drawing blood immediately and knocking her to the sand. She saw the barnacled rock resting on the sand near her eye level. She was totally confused about its origins. How could a rock suddenly hit her as she sat by the fire in a protective hollow? As she struggled to her feet another missile landed with a painful thud against her upper arm, while another barely missed her head soon after.

Louise covered her head as a shower of rocks descended upon her from the bushes bordering the campsite. One struck her head a vicious blow nearly rendering her unconscious before Mark finally stepped clear of his camouflage. He continued to rain down smaller rocks upon her prone body as he advanced.

"I told you to leave my stuff alone. Get the fuck out of here, bitch!"

"Mark, stop it, have you gone nuts? You hurt me."

"How does it feel? Not nice, is it? Now get out and don't come back. I am not going to share with you. Find your own food and water just like I had to."

"Mark you have to stop this, we need each other. I could help you."

"No, we don't need each other. You might need me, but I don't need you. I realise I have never needed you. Everything was always you pushing and manipulating me to get what you wanted. Well, I don't need you and I certainly don't want you, so do us both a favour and just get lost."

"Mark, you can't mean that? You can see that I need help, that before long I'll be waddling with this pregnancy. You have to help me, Mark, please? I, I won't survive without your help. I know I did the wrong thing and I'm really sorry, but you have a moral obligation, if not a legal one, to help me."

"Oh, I see, you think you can hit me up with a legal suite on a negligence basis when we get out of this, huh? Gee, that's going to win me over that is. I'm trembling in my lawyer shoes now, Weesie! Remember how I said that it would be easy enough to kill you then bury you somewhere. Nobody is going to dig up the place looking for you if I say I saw no one else the entire time I was here. I am not kidding about this. I hate your guts and I don't care if you live or die. I am not going to help you, especially because you are pregnant! There is no point trying to play that sympathy card because you forfeited all rights to sympathy the second you told me you were pregnant with someone else's child. Don't you understand that?"

"Yeah, yeah, I get that, Mark, but you don't understand…"

"I don't have to understand, I don't have to listen, and I don't have to do a fucking thing you ask. What you have to do is go before I really hurt you. I want you totally gone, out of my life forever. I don't ever want to see or hear from you again. Take your whiney voice someplace else. Live, die, whatever. I don't want to know."

"I have to explain something to you, Mark."

"Don't want to hear it, not interested."

"No seriously, Mark, I really do have to…"

"No! You have five seconds to get out of here before I start throwing rocks again, and I won't miss your head from this distance."

Louise backed away slowly shaking her head in disbelief. She couldn't believe what she was hearing or seeing. It was not the same person she fell in love with at all. Mark had changed into…a lunatic, a psychopath! There was a deadly gleam in his eyes that brooked no argument, sent shivers down her spine, yet she knew she had to engage his help to survive.

The baby's survival was all she cared about, but that meant she had to survive for a time as well. She had important information to deliver to Mark, information that might reverse his opinion of her, or at the very least, lessen the hostility. If she could just sit with him for a few moments in a calm state to discuss the matter, they may be able to work something out together.

Mark wouldn't listen, though. She didn't seem to be able to penetrate the poisonous shield he'd created. Only one other possibility presented itself as an option. Not the option she would have chosen unless desperation demanded it. She stopped walking backwards. She smiled confidently while taking off her rags.

Mark's smirk turned into hysterical laughter.

"Oh, the sex ploy? Good one, Weesie. Yeah, why not? Now you're turning tricks for food and warmth, which makes sense. Nothing is beneath you, is it? Can't get what you want by stealing it or talking your way into it, you'll just offer up sex to get it. Have you seen yourself lately? Not that I really care what a girl looks like all that much, after all, I close my eyes during sex, but there is no way I would allow my body to enter those infested waters again. You look like shit and you have had that filthy bastard's prick in you while you were engaged to me. I wouldn't touch you with a barge pole let alone *my* pole. Now go, fuck off for good. You disgust me, you fucking slut. LEAVE."

Mark pointed the way down the beach before rearing back with a rock in his outstretched arm, poised to throw at her should she refuse to go. Louise gathered her rags to her front protectively covering herself as best she could, while she turned to walk back the way she came without further comment.

She knew she was beaten, that Mark was no longer in full control of himself. She would not be able to talk to him and make him understand that she truly did have something important to tell him. Nothing she told him now would be heard by his ears. She knew how far his hatred had eaten away at him while he was on the atoll, with no one to turn to for wisdom or solace. Mark was losing his mind as far as she could tell and had become a danger to her as well as himself. She would not return or she may never survive to tell the tale.

She trundled up the beach forlornly, clutching her rags to her bosom, crying tears of frustration and pity for herself and Mark. She tried to stem the blood oozing slowly from her damaged chin. She didn't think she could survive until help arrived. She was mostly sorry for the child who would not live to return home.

Mark watched her go, elated and distraught simultaneously. He had lain in wait to trap the Rat and sure enough, it showed up. She looked bad enough from a distance but he could not quite believe the extent of her deterioration once she came close. He felt bad. Guilty. The forces in his brain were twisting him this way and that. Rage had dwelt in him so long that it was impossible for him to let it go. He pitied her.

Not enough to make him change his plans, though. The Rat had to be punished for encroaching on his home. No way could he let the Rat escape its due. He had watched her every move, including the way she set herself up to keep an eye on the beach for signs of his departure and arrival. How stupid she was to think he could not outsmart her. He hadn't survived as long as he had without some serious smarts happening upstairs.

He had to learn so much from scratch about first-aid and living off the land, making fire with nothing but a pair of granny glasses, and making himself a reasonably comfortable bed and building a roof overhead. He made a home for himself within the harsh climate of this desolate atoll, alone for over two months. No one was going to take anything away from him that he had to fight for with blood, sweat, tears, and a load of pain.

Besides, Mark didn't want anything to do with the woman who dumped him just before a plane blew up! What did she think, that he was a masochist? His name was not the Marquis De Sade and he didn't like pain of an emotional or physical nature, thank you very much. Mark hurled the last stone he had been clutching in his hand, in her direction. The stone fell well short of its target, but Mark didn't care. As long as his ploy worked and he was rid of her for good...he supposed? He had longed desperately for company, someone to share his burdens. He hoped beyond hope that someone else may have survived the wreck. Why her? He needed someone who could help with their situation, not burden him more. He could hardly provide for himself. No way could he provide for her and her bastard brat when it came.

He hoped he would not be around at that time anyway. Surely a boat would come by soon? He knew he was losing it slightly and didn't want to be a total nut job when they eventually rescued him.

YEAR EIGHT

"Happy Birthday, Louie, you little bastard. How old are you? Yeah, eight, that's right. Show me in the sand, show me the number eight, boy."

With deft little hands, the eager young boy scribed a large figure eight in the sand for his beloved Uncle Mark. He looked up for confirmation with an enormous, trusting grin.

"Yep, you got it, boy. I really need to make more time for your lessons though, Louie. I've been pretty damn lax about that. You wouldn't make the grade back home."

"Home?" asked Louie peering toward their camp with a puzzled expression.

"No, not that one boy. The one you've never seen, where you were conceived."

"Con…?"

"Conceived, Louie. You were born here, but you were not con…made here. You were made by two people across the sea in Australia like I've told you about a thousand fucking times you little bastard. When are you going to get it? This putrid little dot on the map is not the world, even though it's all you've ever known, boy. Someday…some-bloody-day, we'll get off this shit of a place and return to Australia and…and… Yeah, and then what genius? I haven't figured that part out yet, boy. Your, Uncle Mark is a bit hazy about the details of his blessed homecoming and the bloody events thereafter. As you are a right little bastard and not my child, I guess you will have to be turned over to the authorities, little man. No more Uncle Mark then, boy, it'll be off to your real dad I reckon. And good bloody riddance to you too is what I say. You're nothing but a bloody nuisance anyway you little bastard. Cheeky, rotten…."

"Cheeky, rotten little bastard," Louie finished for him beaming from one ear to the other. They played this word game often and Louie knew every single one of his uncle's euphemisms for him.

Mark smiled amiably at the tyke. He had tried for eight long years to hate the little bastard, coming close at times, but never quite achieving the venom he desired. From the moment he cut open the mother to release the squirming little monster, Louie had inveigled his way into Mark's good graces first, then slowly, his heart.

He could not hate the boy for the sins of the mother or father. True they were brutal, testing years in which he often thought he might end up killing them both on numerous occasions. The difficulty of bringing up a baby in the harsh environment was the ultimate test of Mark's patience, skill and endurance.

Mark watched Louie run off to play naked at the edge of the surf. He was finding it harder and harder to get the boy to keep any clothes on. He grew out of everything Mark made for him so fast, that it hardly seemed worthwhile remaking any damn thing at all.

His bronzed, super-healthy appearance belied the fact that melanoma could be starting deep within the epidermis. His supply of sun cream had run out long ago. They were at the total mercy of the sun, so Mark knew a battle was looming to keep the boy covered while exposed.

For eight fucking years the boy had been with him like a second skin, never venturing too far, never giving him cause to regret his decision. At least lately, that is. In the beginning, it was a bloody nightmare. How he managed to overcome his repulsion to cope with rearing a bastard child was still a mystery to him.

Those first few months when life swayed in the balance so precariously had left Mark exhausted, emotionally and physically. His leg had healed admirably by that time with only a slight limp noticeable on colder mornings. It was fortuitous that his mobility had much improved because it would be tested many times over during those incredibly stressful first months. He remembered clearly the ominous sound of tortured screams echoing through the night eight years ago.

At first, he thought he might be imagining things as he lay awake trying to distinguish what he heard over the sloughing breeze rustling through the palm fronds. He sat up when at last he knew that it was more than the wind or animal, or any other familiar sound. A distant, though persistent scream of agony penetrated the otherwise still night. Neither the waves lapping gently at the shore nor the coconut wind chimes could drown out the unmistakable sound of a human in great distress.

That human, of course, had to be Louise. She was the only other inhabitant of their tropical 'paradise'. He debated long and hard with himself whether to attend to the urgency of the sounds or simply ignore them as he told her he would.

He had relented back when she was still the Rat. Despite his every desire to maintain the hate and keep his distance, he just wasn't able to do nothing.

"Louise," he shouted as he stood awkwardly near her place of concealment on the dunes.

"What?" she asked as she slowly crept into view.

"Don't ask me why I am doing it, and don't try to get more from me. Every second day, I will place some food and water here if I have enough. No guarantees. I have no way of knowing if I can get food every day, or water. I don't want you in my camp. I can't handle that, not after what you did to me. I, I'm not sure about...not sure my mind is all that stable. Some days are worse than others and I've started talking to myself, a lot. You hurt me, Louise. I try to tell myself that I never really loved you, but I know that's a lie. I can never forgive you, though. That is just...not in me."

"I'm sorry, Mark. I truly am."

"Doesn't help any. The damage was done. Take my offer or leave it, just stay away from my camp, I mean it."

He never spoke to her again after that. She found her way through the interior of the island back to her shack and returned every two days to retrieve the meagre morsels of food and water left for her by him. Over the months that followed, his sanity wavered more and more. He spoke to himself, the island, anything that moved. He argued with and cursed his unseen companions constantly.

In the end, it was more curiosity than any goodwill that saw Mark venturing through the middle of the atoll to make his way to the shack on the exact opposite side. He knew the way well, as he had made the trek many times to keep tabs on her without her knowledge. Or so he believed.

He begrudgingly had to pay Louise her dues, for she managed to survive somehow despite the towering odds. She even looked semi-acceptable at times when he secretly spied on her, often masturbating when he saw her bathing nude. She kept her body reasonably clean and found some more dresses somewhere, which she wore most times to prevent sunburn.

Her blonde, sun-bleached hair grew longer over the months. He watched as she waddled toward the water each day. She was heavy with the pregnancy, all out front, causing her great discomfort. He guessed she had learned some of her survival skills from observing him for a time. At least she observed him from a distance and never once came back to his camp. He was very sure of that, very pleased. He would have followed through with his promise had she ignored him. Mark was not proud of that fact but wasted no time over it either. 'It is what it is', he kept reminding himself.

The moon shone brightly in the cloudless sky as Mark made his way through the dense foliage along the well-used path they had forged over time. The screams grew louder the closer he came. More than once Mark decided to turn around, only to change his mind before doing so. He guessed that it was time for the baby to arrive, that Louise had gone into labour with her bastard child.

He still hoped that neither would survive the ordeal, but walked on regardless. He kidded himself that it was only curiosity and nothing more that made him take the journey. He was adamant that he would not render assistance in any way, he merely wanted to witness her ultimate demise.

He assumed the atoll would feast on more human remains before the night was old. Better her than him, that's for sure. Bloody atoll tried pretty hard to get him all right, but he had conquered every challenge so far. He didn't want to test himself further, though.

Long ago Mark knew of a family of feral pigs on the atoll, remarkably, able to sustain their livelihood on the bleak landscape. He often heard them squealing at night at varying distances from his camp. He knew it was not the pigs on this night making the noise that woke him. The unmistakable sound was that of a human in mortal agony. He supposed it was what any maternity ward sounded like with pregnant mothers in the throes of labour. He did know that labour could take a long time if movies and books were to be believed, so he was prepared for a lengthy vigil from his secret location among the shrubs on the perimeter of the area bordering the shack.

His usual vantage point gave him a clear line of sight to within the shack where she had made her nest out of woven palm-frond mats on the floor. From there he could make out the silhouetted form of her lying on her back atop the mats. He settled back to observe as he nibbled on a few tidbits he had taken along for the show.

Her long wailing screams pierced the still night, rendering the usual menagerie silent. He could make out that she was becoming fatigued with the enormous effort of withstanding labour pains hour after hour.

Her screams diminished with every passing hour until mere whispers of breath escaped, as the sun began to rise majestically in the east. When all remained silent for more than ten minutes, when he could discern no movement from the prone form on the floor, Mark raised himself cautiously from his hideout.

As quietly as possible he made his way to the entrance of the shack where the door hung askew on hinges that had long ago departed from the door frame, leaving but one screw at the bottom to hold the door in place.

He entered the darkened space with mixed feelings of relief and concern that it was all over. He could not contain his curiosity, though. He had pictured it so often in his dreams, day and night. His revenge was at hand at last, and he didn't want to miss the opportunity to witness his victory. His heart raced as he neared the body illuminated by the few narrow beams of sunlight penetrating the shack through the many holes in the roof and walls.

As he bent down to say his final goodbye to her, he nearly suffered a heart attack as the body moved slightly. She had opened her eyes, watching him through fluttering lids. He clutched his heart with startling dismay and was about to rush out when he heard a strained, strangled voice.

"B-b-breech. B-b-baby is…side. Cut, Mark. Cut…b…out.'

"I don't understand what you're saying, and I'm not here to help anyway, so…"

"Cut…baby…out!"

'Are you out of your mind?'

Louise had lapsed into unconsciousness and was unable to answer. Mark was terribly confused and distraught. He didn't want to be involved in anything to do with the baby or her, least of all assist in any way.

What was she talking about anyway? Did he hear right? Did she really want him to cut the baby out of her? No, she couldn't possibly mean that, could she? Breech, she said. A breech birth.

He had heard of that somewhere. It meant, as far as he remembered, that the baby was not aligned head first facing the birth canal, that the baby was side-on. If it was a cow, a veterinarian would probably stick his arms into the cow to turn the calf around, but he didn't have that option.

Shit! He was thinking wrong. He should not have been thinking about options, he should have been hightailing it out of the shack back to his camp until the whole sordid mess resolved itself. His hesitancy proved only that he was considering options, a state of mind unfamiliar to him after hating her for so long.

His brain was addled into immobility and confusion. He was unable to compartmentalise the conflicting emotions to deal with the emergency. He was incapable of determining his correct response according to the dictates of his experiences. While he felt pity, his beleaguered brain refused to allow him to relent in his negative feelings for her. It had just been a way of life for him for so long that he had become accustomed to it. It was natural for him to feel great resentment for her. His confusion saw him mumbling to himself as he trod tight circles within the shack.

A cry of intense anguish disrupted his mosaic of raging thoughts. Louise was still alive and he could see waves of movement from the distended stomach. It would be so easy he thought, just leave, and let it all play out the way it should. Not his problem and never was. Her fault entirely for dumping him, and all her baggage *onto* him.

He cried with rage and frustration. Sheer pent up emotions swirling about him in ever-tightening spirals until he was overcome with the complexity of it all.

Indecision thwarted his every move. Every nerve-ending was frayed to beyond endurance with the intensity of the moment, awash with uncertainty. No courtroom battle was ever as cataclysmic as this event. No comparison in the pure gut-wrenching, emotional turmoil in which he found himself.

Her whimpering interrupted his tumultuous thoughts once more. He had to make a decision very quickly, before…before what? Before he chickened out is what. Before it was too late to do anything at all, which he was secretly hoping. He wished with all his might that the decision could be taken from him. That she would just perish, along with the bastard child within. He could then return to his camp and resume his life in wait. But no, she had to go on living like some kind of continuing horror story. A non-expiring villain, able to return episode after episode to shock audiences further.

He hated himself for the doubt and uncertainty he displayed. He tried desperately to banish the thoughts he had of rendering assistance to the nether regions of his mind, where they might be locked away for good. His usual clarity of thought, of pragmatic direction, was displaced by an inept feeling of disquiet, disillusionment, and inadequacy.

Thrusting aside everything that occurred after the fateful day of the crash, Mark removed his tiny nail clipper blade from his backpack. Worn almost uselessly thin from all the sharpening on rock surfaces, Mark looked at the pitiful thing with contempt.

He had no fire with which to sterilise the blade, no suture material to sew the wound. In fact, he had nothing at all to render the type of assistance required. He would ultimately be responsible for her death if he proceeded. The bloody baby would not live long in any event. He had no means with which to keep the baby alive should he successfully remove the bloody thing in the first place.

Moaning with the forces warring within him, Mark kneeled by Louise's still form. Sweat oozed from her every pore, befouling the air with its stench. Mark assumed the cut would have to be near the top line of her pubic hair or thereabouts. A lateral incision he supposed rather than a vertical one, though what gave him that idea he could not guess.

He winced as he sawed away at the tough human flesh resisting his hideously blunt instrument. He was trying very hard to cut through the flesh and muscle without cutting too deep, thereby causing injury to the baby squirming beneath. Blood trickled from the open wound as Mark penetrated the layers. Louise's heart rate had slowed so much that less blood than expected flowed from the incision.

Once the incision reached a certain length, a membranous bulge protruded through the opening. Soon thereafter, the entire squirming lump fell out of the aperture into his arms. Clearing away the mucous from the infant's mouth allowed the first breath of pure air to intrude upon the boy's lungs. He convulsed and coughed his annoyance at the ghastly invasion to his fluid-filled normality, incensed at the release from his warm, comfortable cocoon.

Mark sat back with the baby cradled in his arms and howling its obscenities to the world at large for being disturbed. The baby was still attached to the remains of the sac via the umbilical cord. Mark knew that he had to cut the cord a little distance from the point of origin at the baby's navel where it needed to be tied off and left to eventually fall off of its own accord, if the infant lasted that long, which was very much in doubt.

The baby eventually settled enough to stop it's howling, sensing his surroundings with his as yet unseeing eyes. Mark inspected the boy for ten fingers and toes, taking particular note of the rather large appendage between his legs. He had not thought of a baby being so well endowed at birth. He felt a little jealous of the father granting the boy such a marvellous weapon.

"Not too shabby for the son of a rat. That makes you a rodent, I suppose. If that thing grows any more, if you get older, then you will put me to shame, mate. Here, let me show you your moth…"

Louise had passed away. The enormous strain of a very long birth and the subsequent operation had finally convinced her exhausted body to quit. Her eyes were closed and her mouth formed the slightest Mona Lisa smile, like she knew that everything was fine, that she was able to leave without regret or concern for her infant.

Mark sat there for what he assumed was a very long time as the enormity of his actions dawned on him. The bundle in his arms nestled quietly against his bare chest, content to feel the warmth of his caregiver and the beat of his heart giving nurturing succour and promise. Mark stared at the boy in his arms with fascination, awe, and bemusement. He had no idea what the future would hold, or how the scenario would play out, but he also was content for the moment to cradle the boy next to him in a warm, wet embrace.

Eight years later, they were celebrating the boy's birthday while still marooned on the atoll. Mark watched as Louie ran along the shoreline, ankle-deep in the waves cascading up the beach in a frothy wake. Always mindful never to venture too far into the water with the ever-present danger of sharks patrolling, Louie ran carefree along the beach with all the exuberance and innocence of an eight-year-old.

Mark watched with the practised eye of a guardian, swelling with pride at the lean, muscled physique already developing in the boy's limbs and torso. Regardless of the lean cuisine to be had on a daily basis, rationing everything constantly, the boy continued to flourish with health and vitality. Their hunting expeditions provided more nourishment than when Mark first arrived, but still, it was a constant battle to feed them both with all the nutrients they required to survive and for the child to grow.

Mark reflected on the enormous responsibility he shouldered when he took the squalling infant back to the camp that fateful night. Panicked, confused and flat out overwhelmed with the preposterous burden he had assumed. His usual state of melancholia plummeted to record depths.

How difficult those first few months were, with Louie never being out of the woods where survival was concerned. Had Mark not cottoned on to the idea of capturing one of the feral sows roaming the island to provide milk for the rodent, it would never have survived the first few days.

Typical of a new arrival to any household, life in the camp was turned upside-down with all his routines completely destroyed, dismantled and strewn asunder. Milking the bloody sow was always an insanely dangerous proposition. Mark flirted with almost certain disaster at each attempt. Then finding ways to transfer the milk to the rodent while still warm and fresh from the teat, was an interesting and frustrating event.

It took almost three days to catch the right animal, one that had recently given birth, before he was able to give the rodent its first decent meal. Before that, he had tried coconut milk warmed as best he could, as well as a little water just to keep it hydrated. The constant bawling during that time drove Mark to near suicide. His frazzled, tired brain was hardly capable of thought let alone a solution to the problem.

When the sow's milk was finally available and he found that simply dipping his finger into the milk to transfer it to the rodent's mouth was the answer, he was able to relax a little. He was furious as hell at the bloody rodent's mother for inflicting him with such an impossible task, but gradually, the infant settled into a semi-contented routine of feeding, burping and the usual bodily functions associated with those activities.

He bundled fragments of old clothing into wads, which he secured with a nappy of sorts, made from woven palm fronds. The wads needed constant cleaning and drying, which kept Mark so busy at times he was unable to provide food for himself. Every waking and non-waking moment centred on the needs of the bloody rodent.

Thoughts of rescue and fires, along with every other planned event faded into obscurity when faced with the daily challenges of keeping the rodent alive, clean, and as happy as possible, because a happy rodent meant less bawling. Always a good thing as there is no sound in all the universe more annoying and penetrating as a bloody infant's bawling. It is a helpless cry of such import that he found himself unable to resist its call.

He found himself waking at the slightest stir during the depths of his sleep, where sleep consisted of only two or three hours at a stretch if he was lucky. A tiny gurgle or unfamiliar movement beside him during the evening saw Mark instantly awake and alert.

The captured sow continued to provide nourishment for the rodent for many months. Sometimes it was hard to tell whose bawling and squealing were louder, the pig's or the rodent's. It was a competition that saw Mark often cringing in emotional turmoil as all he wanted to do was end it, them, run away, anything for his quiet camp once more.

Keeping the sow fed and secure was a full-time job on its own. Ensuring the pig's relatives didn't affect a rescue also demanded constant attention. The drift of pigs with its farrow of piglets ventured alarmingly close on numerous occasions attempting to locate and free their missing relative, or at the very least punish the culprits responsible for its disappearance. He often had to guard the camp with a burning branch to dissuade the feral pigs from gaining access to the sow's pit enclosure.

Those were times he would rather forget for all the trouble they caused him, yet, Mark felt himself softening over time. His inner rage had demurred to a gentle dissatisfaction with the mother's behaviour. His temper quickly tamed by the trusting rodent looking upon him with unashamed fondness. The cooing nature and brilliant smiles of the baby eked away at Mark's frosty façade, finding root in the inner spaces, the kind nature Mark had kept at bay for so long.

The feeding times became moments of pure bonding, only possible between infant and guardian. The tranquillity of the camp at a midnight feeding while sitting by the smouldering fire under an impossible canopy of stars, soothed the savage beast in them both, marking an unmistakable, unbreakable connection deep inside their respective psyches. Holding the rodent to his bare chest, feeling its tiny heartbeat, its precious warmth and the sweet sound of sucking nourishment off his finger, gave Mark a new meaning to his existence.

With every month the rodent managed to survive amid the harsh conditions, the stronger the bond became, though Mark always kept up the uncaring charade in his dialogue. He always retained a debasing vocabulary by calling the boy a rodent, or a bastard, or any other profanity that entered his mind at the time.

He had to maintain the outward appearance of disenchantment with the boy and his mother to appease the Devil within. He would not forsake the antipathy entirely. The fragments of hostility had to remain as a perpetual reminder to him of the gross injustice inflicted upon him by the Rat. He vowed never to forsake that little bit of a defensive nature to guard against times of emotional trauma to come. If they were rescued, much would be undone. Their relationship would alter drastically, perhaps be severed permanently. He needed to keep a certain detachment alive to survive such an outcome.

Days turned to weeks, to months, to years, as the two grew up together to face the daily struggle of survival and a developing relationship amid the uncertainty of their future. Mark worried incessantly of the dangers surrounding them, the natural elements of sun and fierce tropical storms spewing lethal lightning bolts at the earth.

Dangers abounded everywhere. Even a simple cut from a barnacle could spell the end if an infection took hold. He worried whether he was providing the right amount of vitamins and minerals required by a growing body or whether the boy would be stunted in some way for lack of certain nutrients. The paramount goal of every day they remained on the atoll, was their health and well-being. Without that, there would be no one left to rescue. He did, however, slowly give up hope that they would succeed in flagging down a passing ship or signalling a plane. He had never seen another one in all the time spent gazing with forlorn hope at the empty horizon.

Mark also worried about the boy's education and the necessary social growth accompanying time spent with other children his own age. He knew that they needed to escape the atoll before trouble occurred, before it was too late. With basically nothing else at his disposal other than a sliver of a nail-clipper knife worn precariously thin with time and some hand-made implements, they lacked the ability to fashion a raft or attempt anything like it.

He would not risk their lives at sea on some half-arsed attempt on a flimsy vessel unable to withstand the rigours of the open ocean. One idea he had yet to implement, was the total exploration of the atoll. He had never fully explored the other side of the atoll where Louise's shack was located. He had judiciously avoided a return journey to the shack since the night he delivered the rodent.

Several reasons prevented him from venturing there, not the least of which was the shallow grave of the rodent's mother. He didn't have the time or the will to dig a sufficiently deep grave the morning the Rat died. The corpse may well have been uncovered by animals or exposed by the driving rains.

The time was around July, with the extreme heat of summer to follow soon after spring. December through to March was close to intolerable at times, with heat so severe that collapse was possible without warning. Heatstroke was a very real threat throughout the long summer months when temperatures could soar, with humidity almost ninety per cent.

It was a constant struggle to impress upon the boy the very real dangers of overexposure to the sun, be that directly or indirectly. Even sleeping in the dappled shade of their camp during the height of the summer noon could burn the skin and dehydrate the body very quickly.

Mark had decided some time ago that a fuller exploration was necessary to determine or discover a means by which to leave the atoll under their own steam, sail, whatever. He had to make sure he had covered every millimetre of the atoll. It was essential to not leave any stone unturned in his efforts to discover a way off.

Their time was finite. It was not a question of if something catastrophic occurred but when. Sooner or later their luck would run out and medical attention beyond their capacity would be required. Mark would never forgive himself if that occurred without him having searched the entire length and breadth of the atoll. He had stockpiled some provisions for the trek, hoping to be successful in finding supplemental food along the way.

He caught a suckling pig a week ago which he butchered roughly with the edge of a shell. He then dried the meat in the blazing sun with smoky fires surrounding the drying racks to keep the flies away. The pork jerky was gamey and chewy but would sustain them for a time. They had enough water to keep them going for a few days with proper rationing. Living off the atoll had become routine in their bay, but would prove more difficult away from their base.

Mark called the boy over to discuss his plans. While the rodent was still very young, Mark preferred to consult him on issues affecting them both. He lacked formal education, yet his ability to hunt, track and provide for their livelihoods was without peer. His education in survival 101 was his first and foremost lesson, continuing to evolve with each new day and experience.

Mark had sharpened the end of a thin sapling which he then tempered in the coals of their campfire. Louie had surpassed Mark by a country mile in its use as a fishing/hunting spear. Though he was as yet unable to throw an appreciable distance, his accuracy more than made up for the shortfall. The rodent seemed to see through the refraction in the water many times better than Mark could accomplish. The rodent even had the temerity to teach Mark the finer points of its use.

"Yes, Uncle?"

"Sit down boy, I need to talk to you about something. Not sure where to start really. Listen, Louie, we have to get off this bloody atoll or we are going to die here."

"I won't let us die, Uncle. I can hunt for more food if you like?"

"You need to shut up now and listen, okay? It's not entirely about the amount of food we have or water. There's a lot of things we have to consider and some of those you won't understand because all you have ever known is this place, this life. What you don't know is the sort of things that can happen to a person, the dangers we face here every day. You have never been sick or hurt badly enough to need anything more than a cleaning of a cut and a simple bandage. I broke my leg badly when I landed here and you can see by my limp that I didn't do a very professional job of setting the bone right. If something like that or worse happens again to me, you aren't going to cope. If something like that happens to you, that you need hospitalisation…"

"Hosp…hospi…"

"Hospitalisation. Don't interrupt me, you little bastard. It means being hurt enough to need a doctor. Yeah, yeah… a doctor, someone who learns to look after people who are sick or hurt. Doctors work in hospitals, which are buildings where lots of people can be looked after all at once. We don't have a doctor here and it's only a matter of time before one or both of us is going to get hurt. Jeez, a quick stab from a pig's tusk could leave a nasty wound which could then get infected. Or you could fall out of a coconut tree, or get bitten by a shark. I want to see you safely home, boy. We need to leave here.

"I want us to start searching the whole atoll for anything that might help us get off here. I have no idea what we might find, but the first thing I want to look at is the shack where you were born to see if anything there will be useful. Don't ask me what I'm looking for. All I know is that we have to look, otherwise, we'll never know if there was anything that could have helped us. So, tomorrow, we head off. We fill the backpack with all our food supplies, we put out the fire at camp so it doesn't set the place alight. Then we track through the interior to your mother's shack.

"I have to tell you, boy that you may get upset when we get to the shack. The Rat…I mean, your mother might be exposed to the elements. Do you understand? Your mother's bones and what's left of her flesh may be in plain sight, dug up by the pigs or washed out by the heavy rains. Either way, I need you to be prepared for the sight. No histrionics okay? Shut-up. No questions either. Sick of bloody questions every time I say something you don't understand. That's another thing, you need to go to school to learn all the things I can't teach. I'm not a teacher and I don't like teaching, so you need to learn other things to make a go of it in life. This shithole is not a suitable place to raise a child. If we wait for a passing ship you may be too old to learn, too set in your ways. So, sharpen your spears, gather your bedroll and spare clothes wrapped in a bundle on the end of your spear, then we will go see what we can see, eh, boy?"

The following morning the two of them set off through the thick interior forging a new path along the overgrown one. Many pig trails crisscrossed their passage forward in the dappled sunlight when dawn broke over the horizon in a dazzling display of intensity, washing away the remaining mists brewing from the previous evening.

The heat of the day would be upon them before long, which was the reason Mark had left camp as early as possible, to ensure they had sufficient cover among the dense bushes. Mark and the boy had begun a routine of sleeping through the hottest part of the day to avoid overexposure. Bad enough the boy refused to wear clothes most of the time, running around like some little savage with his spear readily at hand.

For all the reasons he had mentioned to the rodent and some he didn't, Mark felt, instinctively, that their time was running short. It was almost like a malaise within him, a festering canker that relentlessly pursued his thoughts, urging him onward, on a quest for escape.

For over eight years he had been content to follow his routines religiously. For the past few weeks, a gnawing disquiet eked its way into his psyche, forcing him to break away from the norm, to give up his comfortable, albeit unforgiving existence. His lawyer mind fought with the illogical thought patterns invading his sense of well-being but didn't win, was unable to quash them. The irregular impulse to remove them from the atoll was an all-powerful compulsion leading him toward he knew not what.

Mark regretted leaving behind all that they had accomplished at their camp, as he didn't believe they would return. He muttered constantly to himself as the shack drew nearer. He didn't want to face the demons haunting the area surrounding the shack and the grave, or worse, his own demons. He silently cursed the Rat for once again luring him to a part of the atoll he didn't wish to see.

The bloody Rat, the bane of his existence was at it again, causing him an ignominy of emotions he thought were behind him. He enjoyed the calmness he had attained once he left the shack so many years ago. He didn't want to revisit those hostilities within and outside himself, yet the closer they got, the more unbalanced he became. A kaleidoscope of dizzying impressions assailing his mind simultaneously, kept Mark grumbling and sometimes shouting at nothing.

Louie, who trailed Mark at a comfortable distance, felt the palpable change taking over his uncle. The tension grew within the humid confines of their green enclosure. The claustrophobic atmosphere enveloping him made him uneasy, though he could not explain why. He heard the sporadic shouts and low mumbles coming from his uncle but didn't understand what caused them. He was very confused about their reasons for leaving the sanctity of their home.

He could not comprehend the other place that Uncle spoke of, the place he wanted to get back to. He was happy with their life at home and upset by any alteration to their routine. He was in two minds about seeing the bones of his mother, because he didn't know what a mother was, or looked like, or what one had to do with him. All he knew was Uncle. No one else existed for him in all the world, and he wanted it to remain that way.

Louie nearly cried when they left their home that morning at first light. He had been on several hunting expeditions with Uncle, but they always returned home. Uncle said that they may never return home, that he wanted to leave their home by the sea. How could that be? They couldn't float like a driftwood log. They would be eaten by the sharks. He didn't like the idea of being eaten, it sounded very painful. Of course, Louie didn't understand the concept of death at his age despite killing a variety of lifeforms for their meals every day. The idea that death could happen to him or Uncle just didn't bear thinking about.

He was very frightened at the prospect of venturing away from his familiar surroundings. Two places that Uncle had always warned him about was the deep water and the dense bushes inland. Despite Uncle's grave warning, here they were, in the middle of the inland bushes which seemed to go on forever. The heat and humidity were overwhelming and it was only mid-morning!

He feared being trapped forever in the seemingly impenetrable foliage that surrounded him, clawing at his skin, snagging his belongings tied in a bundle on the end of his spear. He wanted to scream loudly at Uncle to stop this foolishness, to return home. However, he knew if he spoke against his Uncle's wishes he would regret it in many ways.

Once, when Louie had been very naughty, Uncle had taken a green branch to his bare backside, which hurt very much but something else frightened him more. He saw the disappointment in his uncle's eyes and never wished to see that look again. He was very ashamed of his actions when they caused his uncle to look at him like that.

Louie would follow his uncle to the ends of the earth, which was not very far in Louie's opinion as he had been there many times on their hunting trips. Uncle had told him that was not the end of the earth, but Louie knew better than silly old Uncle.

The earth stopped at the water and the water went on forever, as far as the eye could see in all directions. He had seen the sun come up from the bottom of the ocean at one side and sink on the other side, so he knew with certainty where the earth stopped because he could see it with his very own eyes. He thought that Uncle might be getting too old to remember things correctly anymore.

Uncle's mind was slipping. He would have to follow Uncle around just to make sure he didn't get lost or hurt himself. The silly talk of finding something to put on the water to get away from their home was a fantasy of his uncle's that he had to indulge for the moment, just until his uncle's head cleared a little.

Louie believed with all his heart and mind that they would not leave home. He had only known the one home for as long as he lived and he could not see why they had to explore the atoll. They had everything they needed at home. All this fuss about finding stuff left him bewildered and anxious. He didn't want to see the other side or go through this thick bush any longer but saw no way of convincing his uncle that they should return until his mind got better. Uncle needed Louie to hunt, scout and provide for them, otherwise, he would not survive on his own, and so Louie followed obediently.

The trek grew hotter as they slogged through the tangled brush that covered the entire inner portion of the atoll. The path Mark had forged through the atoll eight years earlier was totally grown over, even thicker if that was possible. It was tough going without some sort of machete or scythe to clear the way. It was exhausting work while making extremely slow progress in the dire heat.

The dappled shade did little to lessen the waves of torrid heat descending upon them with the rising sun. Mark knew that they were not able to make the trek during the much preferable cool of the evening as he did so long ago, because the track no longer existed. They would flail about blindly if they left at night. Huge spiders were also a constant worry when they came across the webs strung between bushes to catch small birds and bats.

Mark could hear Louie grumbling softly behind him, unaware that his uncle could hear him. He felt sorry for dragging the rodent through the jungle of bushes and undergrowth but knew they had no option. Instinct told him, screamed at him if truth be told, to find a way off the atoll. He had learned during his time marooned, to allow for the fact that forces other than logic ought to be given their fair share of consideration. Those illogical thoughts, at times, saved him from making decisions that would have proven disastrous had he ignored them. He learned to regard them more often with an open mind, a non-lawyer mind when they presented themselves. One specific incident came to mind when he thought about such things.

Louie was about three or four, playing around a pool among the rocks at the point where he caught the crayfish. Without knowing exactly why, he rushed to Louie's side suddenly, snatching him up into his arms before he could step into the pool with his bare feet. No sooner had he held Louie above the water when he saw a small stonefish move from its hiding place within the pool right where Louie was about to step. The sting from the fish would have been deadly to someone as young as Louie.

Maybe he had seen a flicker of movement in his peripheral vision, maybe not, he couldn't be sure. What he did know, was that he saved Louie's life by acting out of pure instinct rather than reasoning the sensation out. It was an alien process for Mark's super linear training to deal with. He no longer fought the mystical impulses that beset him from time to time. He allowed himself to be gently persuaded by the intuitive machinations of the brain.

Some would call it a sixth sense he supposed but he mistrusted the mysticism surrounding it, giving more credence to the theory that, what primitive man once had in abundance, modern man had forgotten during the progression. Primitive man may well have been more vigilant as well, which afforded him the ability to see all things at once in any environment.

By mid-afternoon, they had reached the shack. Mark sighed with relief when he spied the undisturbed shallow gravesite. He didn't wish to deal with the anxiety involved in witnessing the deterioration of the human form after years of decomposition and animal interference. The scene at the shack brought memories of the birth and death to the surface, escaping from the darkness into which the memories were corralled so long ago.

He shivered involuntarily at the images attacking his mind, stirring up the uncontrolled hatred he felt back then. The unmitigated loathing he harboured for the Rat had been subdued for so long that the return of those emotions frightened Mark with their intensity. He was unsure how he came to feel such animosity toward someone to whom he had once declared his undying love and affection.

The hostility he had nurtured during those long months alone matured into a tangible wrath that obliterated all normal thought. He knew that he had crossed the boundaries of sanity back then. Knew, that perhaps, the boy had saved *his* life rather than the opposite.

It was a revelation that didn't sit well. To him, he felt justified in all his actions from the moment he woke on the beach strapped to the seat. Truth be told, however, he could see that justification was a tool of the guilty to help them diminish their responsibility. He had seen it often enough with clients who attempted to justify all their heinous crimes on the basis of other people's actions which they perceived to be tainted. 'Course I stabbed him, he was lookin' at my woman.' 'Fuck yeah, the bastard had it comin'. 'Just a fucking junkie anyway.' All the different ways of diverting blame away from themselves, Mark had witnessed over and over again. He knew he was deluding himself if he believed he was not culpable in part, if not in full, for the death of the R…Louise.

Despite the animosity he felt, he had a moral obligation to assist a fellow human being to survive. Although Louise had managed to help herself to a certain extent, she would have managed far better if he had allowed her to remain with him. The years had stripped away the cloudiness of his perceptions to reveal the painful truth that he, Mark, had aided, if not caused the death of his fiancée, Louise.

Tears welled unbidden in his eyes as the horrible truth descended upon him like a tidal wave. The sensations he felt as he approached the shack receded into oblivion as the new revelations manifested themselves. While it was true that he had no option at the time, to operate on Louise to remove the baby, it might not have come to that had he been with her during the labour. He was guilty of taking a life, the life of a human being, one he had professed to love.

His shame enveloped him like a death shroud. He was numb to the core. Louie was shouting something at him that he was unable to hear amid the crushing accusations of his guilt and remorse. He crumbled to the sand in a blubbering heap, sobbing plaintively for forgiveness from the mound of sand bearing Louise's remains. Mark felt the world upon his shoulders, the weight of guilt crushing him slowly into the sand. He was unable to control the anguish he felt, the utter shame that caused his body to convulse with torment.

Almost ten minutes passed before Mark was fully spent from the exertion, heaving hollowly with a pained heart. He squatted there, a stricken man incapable of movement or sound. Thankfully, Louie had not pressured him for answers. The boy sat by him with a look of deep concern on his features.

Louie sensed that his uncle was very sad and needed some time. He didn't attempt to talk to him or ask foolish questions that might make him sad again, so he waited by Uncle's side patiently, offering no more than the merest contact.

Mark slowly came to his senses, albeit with deep melancholia settling in for permanent residence. He was deeply ashamed of his actions that led to Louise's ultimate demise, and he bore the full brunt of the guilt associated with that fact. It would not alter the present, nor could he undo the past, so he gradually came to terms with the reality before him.

They must continue their search to find a way off the atoll before it was too late. He turned to smile gratefully at his loyal companion. He had given the boy his name as a way of appeasing the boy's mother and father. Luke and Louise became Louie several months after he was born. Until that time, he was unsure if the child would survive and called him Rodent more often than not anyway. The boy didn't deserve that. At the boy's mother's gravesite, he promised himself to care for the boy better, to respect his individuality and his birthright. He owed it to Louise and Luke to bring their child back to Australia.

"Louie, time to go, buddy."

"Uncle?"

"Yeah?"

"What is, 'buddy'?"

'Friend, Louie. 'Buddy', means you are my good friend. I'm very happy that we saved each other, my friend. Without you, I obviously would have ended up a total fruitcake. This is where I buried your mother, Louise. She would have been an excellent mother had she survived, and I know for a fact, she did everything in her power to ensure your wellbeing. Right up to the very last second, she only had your survival on her mind. You would not be here if it were not for the pure determination and the tenacity of that woman. She swallowed every bit of pride and dignity she possessed to persuade me to deliver you. She died as a result of a very long labour and blood loss from the operation I performed. She had a smile on her face when she breathed her last. I'm sure it was because she saw you in my arms and was able to let go only when she knew that you were going to be cared for."

"Uncle, you never told me this before. What does operation mean?"

"Not now, Louie, okay? I'll tell you the whole story another time. Everything from go to woe, including before being marooned. I owe you that much, boy, and I owe, Louise much, much more. For now, we've got to continue our search. I promise you, Louie, that I intend to find a way off this bloody atoll, to get you back to where you belong. You and I, mate, we are getting back to good old Aussie come hell or high water."

After searching the entire area surrounding the shack, Mark determined that there was little of salvageable use to their goals. He decided to go from there onto as yet uncharted territory. Neither he nor Louie had ever ventured much further than their bay on their hunts. Exploring far inland was next to impossible and travelling too far along the beach took them too far away from known food sources. Besides trapping the occasional pig with its inherent risks, there was little to entice the duo away from their sanctuary that provided semi-adequate provisions for existence.

Louie, of course, revelled in the adventure once free of the inland growth, despite his reservations about leaving their home. He firmly believed they would return once the exploration was out of his uncle's system. Nothing would dissuade him from that train of thought, anything else was simply too impossible to regard.

As evening drew near, the weary travellers approached a hollow behind the dune at the top of the beach. They decided to make camp for the evening, starting a fire from the slow-burning torch Mark had devised out of coals and moist green leaves.

There was just enough heat left to trigger the brittle leaves and coconut fibres he placed on top while blowing gently to reactivate the embers. They dined on smoked pork jerky and water, which suited them just fine as they sat beside the warming fire with a star-filled sky shining brightly above them.

Despite the weariness Mark felt from his emotional distress earlier that day, the long trek along the beach which worried his gammy leg, and the fact that he already told the boy 'another day', he found himself relating to Louie the full story from start to finish. Mark talked long into the evening with Louie hanging on to every word, fighting with himself to contain the many questions that formed in his mind with each new revelation.

As Mark drew near the end of his recollections, to a point near the present, he glanced over to see Louie gradually falling asleep with heavy eyelids, threatening to close any second despite the boy's best efforts to forestall the event. Mark settled the boy lovingly on his matting before settling near Louie on his own matting. They both fell asleep instantaneously.

NINE HOURS LATER

Breaking camp at the crack of dawn saw the two intrepid explorers trekking along the beach in companionable silence, each digesting the new auspices of their relationship in their own private space. Mark felt an overwhelming sense of relief at having unburdened his conscience by telling Louie everything, without bias, allowing the boy to arrive at his own conclusions in his own time.

It was a mighty large block of information for the boy to deal with, so he gave him all the time necessary. Louie was slowly sifting through everything his uncle said with his young, inexperienced mind as best he could. He could not decide whether his uncle, whom he loved beyond anything he had ever known, was actually a bad man or not. He wrestled with himself over the facts as he saw them, what he knew to be true by having witnessed events himself, what appeared to be true if using logical deduction and reasoning, and what, if anything, didn't sound true.

Louie came to the conclusion that his uncle was telling the truth. Louie knew it was a difficult decision for his uncle to make, considering the possible ramifications. He risked losing Louie's affections and loyalty with such startling revelations. Louie didn't believe that Uncle would do so without very good reason, and without everything he said being true.

He had not known about fathers and mothers before his uncle spoke about it, knew very little about anything it seemed, the more he heard. He began to think that maybe, visiting this Australia might not be a bad thing if he could learn some more about all the strange things he didn't know. His heart was torn between the comfortable existence they shared and knew, and the magnitude of the unknown in a foreign land with many, many people.

Louie feared the plan Uncle had in mind, of finding some way to float on water, to travel across the top of sharks and other dangerous creatures of the sea. He didn't like the idea one little bit but saw no other way to reach the land his uncle spoke of. The other thing Uncle mentioned, how he and his mother arrived on the atoll, was too ridiculous to even consider. Louie knew it was his uncle's way of playing with him. To Louie's young mind there was simply no way a flying machine could carry anything, let alone people, over the water.

That part of the story made Louie smile every time he thought of it. It was a very funny joke his uncle was having with him, a way of breaking the horrible story up into an acceptable tale. To Louie, Uncle, and his mother must surely have always been on the atoll from the beginning of time. He had never heard another human being and saw no evidence that others existed, yet Uncle said that many people lived in this Australia and that it was only one of many continents around the world where other people lived.

Perhaps there were other people, but that there were more than he could count on his hands and feet was a preposterous notion. *Silly Uncle, making up strange and wonderful stories for his benefit.* Although they were amusing, they could not possibly be true, yet Uncle didn't look as though he were fibbing. Louie deliberated so hard on the conundrum that he missed seeing the protrusion in the sand, stubbing his bare toe painfully.

Mark stopped to give comfort to the boy who seemed to have tripped on a rock. He had done the same on more than one occasion, as the beach was often littered with pumice and coral pieces amid smaller rocks and such. Even a large shell protruding from the sand could cause a nasty gash or abrasion. As far as Mark could see, there was no serious injury to Louie's toe, just a little bruising that would eventually show.

He was about to get back underway when he happened to glance a second time at the cause of Louie's mishap. Had he not noticed a fleck of colour on the surface he would not have bothered with it in the least. On closer inspection, despite Louie's insistence that it was nothing to concern themselves with, Mark discovered more of the bluish colouring after digging around it some more. A faint recollection gnawed at him as he continued to dig around the growing object. When he had dug a little more, a triangular prism of metal showed above the excavation, and then Mark believed he knew the identity of the object.

It was the corner of a shipping container. He saw no reason to doubt his assumption. The further he dug the more metal he revealed and more blue paint became visible among the rusty sections. The metal had not yet rusted all the way through, though, it was very thin in some areas.

The soft sand at the edges of the hole continued to cave in, making any further progress an impossible task. With the tide resuming its inward cycle, it would not be long before the container was covered once more. It would take some serious contemplation if they planned to explore the possibility that the object actually contained anything at all, useful or not.

The effort to dig the container out to the point where the doors were accessible was a mammoth task in itself. Finding a way to get the door open if, in fact, it were a sealed container, was a task equally immense. Finding anything of use to them inside the container, if all that effort to come to fruition, was a complete unknown. If all the impossible were achievable, then they faced the very real possibility that everything inside the old container was contaminated by seawater to the point where it would be entirely useless. Mark didn't believe that to be the case, though. Evidently, the container floated to the atoll once dislodged from the ship. That indicated a sealed container.

Hell, the damn thing may have tractor parts, paper wine bags, or even Christmas decorations, making his deliberations superfluous. Endless possibilities crowded Mark's mind as he pondered the potential gains against the obvious expenditure of vital energy. The ends may not justify the means. The probability that the container would not hold anything of assistance was so huge that Mark retreated to the top of the beach to set up camp for the evening.

He and Louie watched as the incoming tide slowly filled their hole with water, then covered the object entirely. Mark considered their options weighing up the pros and cons with great deliberation. Many hours, days of effort could be taken up with the fruitless task while their expedition was abandoned or postponed. Wasting precious time and limited provisions whilst gambling on what the container held, didn't sit favourably with Mark.

One thing in their favour seemed to be that the container's doors faced up the beach with the top right-hand corner being the protruding snub that assaulted Louie's toe. The negative view was that they had a maximum of three to four hours with which to complete the task of entering the container before the returning tide covered it. If they were lucky enough to have lower high tides, they may have a little more time with it.

They might have to wait for those periods of king tides to have any chance at all. It would take three to four hours just to uncover one door. Then the problem of dealing with the resilient seal if indeed it was a full container. Mark believed he may have the solution for that particular problem, however. Once the door was opened they would have one, possibly two hours maximum to deal with the contents.

If whatever was inside the container was labelled clearly enough, in English, then they would have to determine its usefulness immediately. If useful, then unloading the container before the tide turned would be crucial. If they failed to empty the container before the tide, they would have to close the door and repeat the entire process the following day. It was not a proposition he cared to think about.

If anything eventuated from the first inspection, it behove them to empty the container to the top of the beach where they could inspect the cargo at their leisure. Mark didn't speculate too long about the contents of the container. His usual premise being, 'it is what it is', continued to be the mantra by which he governed all decisions. He would discuss it all with Louie as well. Louie had to have a say in the investiture of his time and energies.

"Louie, my boy, we have a little conundrum to discuss. That there is a shipping container. It is a large metal box used to transport cargo upon the sea by way of an ocean-going cargo vessel. These large ships carry thousands of these containers in one go across the ocean from one country to another. It's anyone's guess as to what might be in that container if, in fact, it has anything in it at all. Containers like that get swamped off ships all the time in savage storms or hurricanes. I don't suppose it's an empty one, but it's not entirely impossible either. So, there is a lot to consider. Should we make the extreme effort to find out what's inside the bloody thing, or not? I don't expect you to know what's involved in making that happen, Louie, after all, you don't even know what one looks like in its entirety.

"Trust me when I say that getting to the door and opening the damn thing is going to be a huge, labour intensive job. Bigger and harder than anything you've done so far, mate. We only have a small window of time in which to do it as well. We have to beat the tide which gives us no more than about four hours max. We have to wait for the outgoing tide, then wait for that to reveal the container again, start digging a hole at about a metre and a half from the object to enable us to get to the door without all the sand collapsing in on us. Then we have to work out how to get inside and remove whatever it is up to the top here before the tide comes back in. That's all. Nothing to it, piece of cake, huh?"

Louie didn't immediately answer Mark as he stewed on the information, such as it was to his limited understanding, and wondering most of all, about cake? He didn't want to disappoint his uncle with a careless answer after he placed such importance on the con…un…drum. Louie was only eight years old, but he was as strong as a boy could be for his age, having had to live off the land and by his wits since birth. He was unsure of exactly how difficult the task was, considering he knew nothing about the size of the buried object. On the other hand, he didn't want to waste a lot of time and energy for nothing. If Uncle didn't know what was inside the strange thing, or *if* he could get inside it, then it seemed confusing that he wanted to. Why not lift every rock they see if that is the case? Why not look under every shell or washed up seaweed for that matter?

"Uncle, I don't know yet. I want to go to sleep and think about it? I still have questions, though."

"You take as long as you like, Louie, and I'll answer all your questions if I can. I may not know all the answers, though. Some of what I say is supposition and pure guesswork based on the available data."

Mark thought that Louie was growing very quickly and showed signs of inherent intelligence belying his youth. He sensed that Louie didn't want to contradict him, but wasn't totally accepting of the plan either. He didn't believe he had the wherewithal to convince the boy of the necessity of leaving the only home he had ever known.

He couldn't impress upon the boy how important it was for two reasons. Firstly - he didn't quite understand the compulsion himself. Secondly - he could not make the boy understand the gravity of their situation if Louie had no understanding of the world at large. He didn't know sickness, or serious injury, education in a school, children his own age, toys…nothing. He was so disadvantaged by his circumstances that Mark had not the least idea of how to impart the information.

Mark peered at the crackling fire, then at Louie curled up on his side, with his back to the warm flames, pretending to be asleep. He knew Louie well enough to know his breathing patterns when he was fast asleep. The boy was obviously thrashing everything out in his mind, trying to come to terms with his crazy uncle's scheme.

When he placed himself in Louie's skin, he understood only

too well how conflicted the boy must feel. Mark was the only role model Louie had known since birth, giving him no comparisons. Mark knew he had not treated Louie the way a true parent would have because of his obdurate hostility. Mark felt deeply for the boy, but never once showed true affection or love in all the years they were together. Mark was truly ashamed of his past behaviour, his inexplicable antagonism toward the boy caused him great unrest.

It was not the boy's fault that he found himself on the atoll, was not even the fault of the boy's mother. Bad luck and happenstance had seen them take a seat aboard a doomed flight. What his mother had revealed may well have been a catalyst for his aggression, but certainly didn't warrant the outright bellicosity he had shown the mother, then the boy.

Louie loved him unconditionally, he saw that. What he felt in return, he was only just discovering. His emotional breakdown at the shack had broken away the walls he had built around himself as protection against any further hurt. The resultant effect of those impassable walls was the fact that he didn't allow himself to get as close to Louie as he should have. He could have been enjoying the better part of his life with a surrogate son, had he the capacity to see further than his own selfish ideals.

He may never again have the opportunity to rear a child, to experience that bond of child and guardian available to him in the present. If he had been thinking clearly, using the intelligence that saw him attain his degree in law, he might have created something of real significance in his life with Louie. Instead, he tossed it all aside for selfish, self-pitying reasons that were beneath him. He crawled over to where Louie lay, curling up behind him with a protective arm draped over the boy's waist.

Louie was stunned, though he didn't move a muscle when he felt his uncle settle behind him. When his uncle wrapped his big arm around him, he tensed slightly at the foreign embrace. He wanted to turn around to ask his uncle why he was acting that way but felt strangely comforted by the closeness. It warmed his insides in a way he had never experienced before.

A million thoughts and sensations collided against one another like flotsam and jetsam caught in an eddy, yet he felt calmly confident that he was safe and secure. He didn't have time to finish his internal investigations before he drifted off into the deepest sleep he had known. He would not remember having a dream that night, only the warm comfort of his beloved uncle giving him succour at a time he desired it.

Louie woke fresh and rested from his slumbers, then placed some wood on the fire to repel the early morning coolness. His uncle was sitting on the other side of the fire with a relaxed smile on his face, watching him closely, scrutinising his every move with admiration it seemed. Something very strange had happened to his uncle after they had left the shack the previous day. All day long, as they walked the beach, Louie sensed the difference in speech and character displayed by his uncle.

There was none of the normal terseness apparent in his behaviour, the abruptness with which he treated Louie every day of his life. His Uncle Mark seemed…softer somehow, amenable to Louie's questions, with none of the animosity he generally exhibited.

"Uncle, can you tell me what happened to you yesterday?"

Mark was not surprised by the question. He admired the boy's maturity in asking. Louie had to decipher a lot of information yesterday. He was then asked a very pertinent question by Mark who was behaving in a foreign manner. Louie showed remarkable perspicacity at requesting more information before divulging his own opinion. Mark smiled as he mulled over the answer, chewing over the circumstances that led to his breakdown before revealing his answer.

"I woke up I think, Louie. I've been a terrible guardian for you, mate. All your life I've been very hard on you, blamed you and your mother for everything bad that happened to me. I was lost in anger and hatred for so long that it simply poisoned me. Yesterday, on the way to your mother's shack, all those bad feelings came back in a big wave. When I saw your mother's grave, it came crashing down on me. I suddenly saw how cruel I had been to, Louise and then you. She was a woman I loved until the time she took drastic measures to overcome her own hurt.

"I took revenge on your mother after she hurt me. I banished her from my life and my camp. I don't know if your mother would have survived childbirth had she been safe with me at the camp but I certainly didn't help her either. I felt…so ashamed and guilty all of a sudden when I saw her grave, guilty that I abandoned her when she needed some help. Even though we were no longer together as a couple, I knew I was obligated to help a fellow human being, but I did nothing.

"I can't ask her for forgiveness, Louie, and I don't deserve your forgiveness for the way I've treated you either. That's why I broke down yesterday. I woke up. I saw the wrong I'd done, and was still doing, to you. I lived with hatred for so long that it became ingrained in me.

"I'll make it up to you if I can, Louie. I don't want anything from you, I want to give something back for everything you've freely given to me all the time we've been together. If you'll allow me, I'll show you some of the affection I feel for you. I've obviously loved you all along, Louie, but by pure stubborn arrogance, I've ignored it, pushed it down, and treated you like I treated your mother to a certain extent.

"For that, I apologise, Louie, with all my heart. I am truly sorry for that. If we ever make it back to civilisation where you can see other children reacting to their loving parents you'll understand what I'm talking about. I love you, Louie, and I should have told you that every day you've been alive because you've given my life more purpose than you'll ever know."

Louie didn't hesitate, he simply ran into Mark's arms where he felt the warm embrace repeated from the previous evening, where he felt the one thing he wanted more than anything in the world, though he was unaware of it the entire time; love and acceptance. He was loved by the man he adored beyond all measure. The man he would follow into the flames of the fire before he should even ask it. His heart swelled with the knowledge, the certainty, that his uncle did feel the connection between them.

His eyes shed tears of pure joy knowing that he belonged to someone, that he was not alone as he often felt at night. He hugged the big man with all his puny might in an embrace he hoped would never end. Louie felt alive, more than at any other time in memory. His senses literally zinged with pleasure as they sat there comfortably in each other's arms. He wanted the moment to continue for as long as possible before he finally broke away to give his uncle an answer.

"Uncle, I think we should do whatever you think is best. You taught me everything I know, and as long as we are together, I think you will do whatever is right for us. I love you too, Uncle Mark. Whatever that means."

Louie smiled an infectious smile about a kilometre wide, which made Mark grin from ear to ear also. Mark explained his plans to the boy, how he intended to obtain access to the container. The boy listened intently, adding his considered opinion from time to time as they waited for the tide to withdraw.

They scoured the beach to find themselves suitable implements with which to shovel away the enormous amount of sand impeding the door's access. The moment the water receded sufficiently, the operation began at a two-metre distance from the protruding corner.

They would have to dig down at least two point four metres according to Mark's memory of a sea container's dimensions. He believed they were usually six metres or twelve metres long, by two point four metres wide by about the same height. Given the angle at which the container was wedged into the sand, they may have to dig deeper than the standard height to free up the door.

Before they started digging he had asked Louie to start a fire on the beach next to the excavation area. They would need a number of logs protruding from the fire, able to be handled easily by them both when the time came. He filled a number of half coconut shells with seawater, which he placed in readiness several metres from the fire, undercover, to keep the water as cool as possible.

Then they both threw themselves into the task with gusto. It was imperative to achieve their purpose on the first attempt, otherwise, everything would have to be repeated for a second try. Mark didn't fancy their chances if they failed on the first two attempts. They would simply be too exhausted to try a third time.

The sweat poured from their backs as the merciless sun beat down upon them in all its tropical intensity. They stopped in their labours only to catch their breath or take a swig of water to keep themselves hydrated. Within a couple of hours, they were getting close to revealing one of the doors. Thankfully, the right-hand door of a sea container needed to be open first before freeing the left-hand door.

If the container were angled the other way it would have required far more labour to free the appropriate door. Mark inspected the intact seal while Louie continued to shovel away the sand covering the lower portion of the door.

As the last of the sand was cleared away to allow access to the door, Mark held a naked flame to the semi-rusted seal locking the door. Both he and Louie took turns in holding the flames beneath the seal until it glowed red hot. At Mark's prearranged signal, Louie gathered the coconut shells containing the cool seawater. Using two of the vessels, he poured the cool water directly on the red hot seal while protecting himself with a driftwood shield.

The seal shattered instantly, showering the pair with lethal splinters. One of which embedded themselves into Louie's big toe. So focused was he, that he hardly noticed the hot sliver penetrate his toe, feeling nothing more than a slight sting. They concentrated on the task at hand and the jubilation they felt at their success.

Using timber levers to pry at the rusted handles on the door, using every ounce of their combined strength, they finally managed to budge the door open a fraction. Jamming more timber into the small opening between the two doors allowed them to lever aside the door sufficiently to see the undamaged contents of the container.

Plain cardboard boxes stacked tightly from floor to ceiling were visible once the door was fully opened. Mark quickly extracted one of the top-most boxes to examine the contents in the absence of understandable writing on the exterior. The box was quite weighty as he began to tear open the lid haphazardly. Both held their breath in anticipation of the contents being revealed and what it could mean to them. The result was somewhat of an anti-climax when Mark spied the pre-packaged metal wood screws within.

Mark was unsure what he had been expecting, but wood screws were furthest from his expectations or wishes. It was a cheap brand of pre-packaged screws with Chinese writing he assumed. He was not able to distinguish one Asian language from another, so assumed that it was maybe a load of cheap stuff heading for a reject store or similar.

His disappointment soon turned to joy with a germ of an idea, when he thought of the possibilities that they may yet discover within the cargo. Mark made the quick decision to unload the entire contents up beyond the waterline near their temporary campsite. Louie didn't have the time or energy to ask the multitude of questions brewing in his mind.

He bent to the task of transferring the contents of the container with positive fervour. Mark and he were on a tight time schedule to empty the container before the tide returned to fill the hole and bury the container once more.

As the last few boxes were hauled safely to the designated area of the beach, Mark closed the door to the container as the first trickles of water cascaded to the bottom of the excavation site with the advancing tide. Within moments the container doors were knee-deep in water.

The labourers withdrew to the temporary campsite where they sat exhausted and numb for some time before they could move. They decided to leave the opening of the boxes for the following morning when they were able to see well enough to determine the use, or otherwise, of the contents. Light diminished swiftly once the sun went down, and they were both so fatigued, that they soon fell asleep after eating a little of their stores.

The next morning, Louie gazed in complete awe at the contents of some of the boxes he tore open with the exuberance of a child on Christmas morning. Mark was still dozing next to the campfire whilst Louie could contain his curiosity no longer. He had absolutely no idea what any of the packaged objects could be, or what they might be used for by anyone, let alone he and Uncle. He eyed each package carefully trying to determine their designated use, but his absence from civilisation left him dumbfounded.

He held an object in his hand with a handle on one end which he assumed one would grip, with a long metal strip protruding from the handle. Along one edge of the metal strip, he could see a line of jagged serrations which were extremely sharp. He made an instinctive sawing motion in the air with the object.

"On the log, Louie. Place that edge on the log in front of you, then do the same thing you just did. Good boy, that's right. It's called a saw, used for cutting wood just like that. When I opened that first box yesterday I was very disappointed. I hoped for, I don't know, for an inflatable dinghy or something equally spectacular and easy. When I thought about the wood screws, though, I had an idea that maybe it was a hardware order which could possibly contain all sorts of goodies including tools just like that saw. One of our biggest problems has been the lack of any tools, even a decent knife. I figure, if there are the right kind of tools in there, we might be able to build ourselves a raft of some kind.'

"You told me about the idea of a raft once but said that we probably don't have the right sort of wood here, Uncle."

"Yeah, you got me there and I still think that's the case. I'll have to think about that some more. We were very lucky that the cargo is intact and that the container didn't leak, otherwise, everything inside would have rusted to buggery. Let's have something to eat, then we'll get to and open all the boxes and place the contents in different piles in order of their usefulness."

By mid-morning, the piles grew as the boxes were opened. Mark had guessed right that it was hardware destined for a store somewhere that sold all the cheap stuff. There were no quality items among the packages. There were many power tools, none of which could possibly assist them as much as Mark wished they might.

There were, however, many hand tools including old fashioned hand drills, which Mark had not seen in a very long time. He didn't know they were still manufactured in this modern age of cordless drills. There were drill bits galore to go along with them, of every imaginable size. There were handheld augers and bits as well for drilling larger holes in poles etc. The pile of useful items soon grew larger than the waste pile. Glues, silicones, and putties all in their prepacked plastic packaging, some hardened with age and discarded, some perfectly preserved for immediate use, were high on Mark's list of useful items.

Polystyrene packaging housing most of the electrical tools would come in extremely handy for floatation purposes along with many boxes of inner tubes for wheelbarrows and the like. The tubes would also make great weapons when used in conjunction with wood which they could now carve efficiently into spears and arrows. They had an assortment of fishing rods, fishing line, hooks, sinkers and lures with which to catch a plentiful supply of fish. Cane cutters and machetes, as well as a selection of utility knives, would give them more capabilities than they had imagined.

But the best prize of all among the many were much-needed matches and firelighters. They need never resort to the pair of glasses again. Many times after storms swept their atoll, had they been forced to revert to lighting a new fire using the glasses, a time-consuming task only manageable in full sunlight. Often the skies remained overcast after storms, which meant that everything remained cold and wet.

Mark was overjoyed with the find. In a worst-case scenario in which they could not build a raft, they would at the very least have the tools and other luxuries to make their lives exceedingly more comfortable. He and Louie held hands and whooped for joy when they finished unpacking all the boxes. Louie was not quite sure why they were so happy, But Uncle's cheer was infectious.

He had never seen Uncle Mark so happy and didn't wish to spoil the occasion with the many questions he had. Mark was simply enjoying the moment to think too far into the future. Many obstacles remained, many problems to overcome before they could make their escape, but at least they had a decent shot. He realised that they didn't have any chance whatsoever beforehand. They were doomed to remain where they were without the miracle find. People would not believe it plausible when they would eventually explain how they escaped their island home.

Their joy was short-lived however when the following afternoon saw Louie pale and sweating. It was the exact scenario Mark feared would occur sooner or later. Louie's rising temperature had Mark very concerned, for there was little he could do to aid the boy other than cold compresses.

Mark tried to figure out what possible illness Louie may have contracted in such a short time. There were no previous symptoms to denote the onset of a flu-like ailment. No coughing, sore throat, headache or any other discernible complaint. Mark explored the possibility of an insect bite or poisonous plant intake. He quickly discarded the poisonous plant scenario as they had eaten nothing out of the ordinary, which left the insect bite theory.

Mark searched Louie's upper body and skull in particular for evidence of a bite mark, tick infestation or other. Then searched lower turning the boy over as gently as possible. His chest and abdomen bore no evidence of marks other than the usual set of bruises and abrasions typical of their time spent foraging for food each day. His groin area and buttocks were clear, as were his legs until he came to the boy's big toe on his right foot. It was tinged with blue and yellow and badly swollen.

Mark inspected the toe as closely as possible but was hampered in his efforts by what he recognised as failing eyesight. He was no longer able to focus accurately up close. He resorted to the use of the old lady's glasses once more which he used as a magnifying glass to inspect the toe.

He soon found the offending splinter embedded deep in the toe, or more accurately, he discovered the entrance site of the foreign object without actually seeing the object itself. The toe was hot and obviously infected. Mark knew that without removing the object, the infection may cause blood poisoning or turn gangrenous. Either scenario would spell the end without medical attention.

Mark was left with no choice but to perform a minor operation to dig the splinter out. He assumed it was a wooden splinter in the absence of any other likely explanation. Luckily they had brand new utility knives with extremely sharp blades among their treasures. He would need to cleanse them of all oily coatings meant to keep them rust-free during disuse.

Louie was half delirious and shivering when the heat left his body. He tossed and turned continually as Mark tried desperately to soothe him. He would have to tie Louie down in order to stabilise the foot enough to operate on the toe.

Using nylon ropes they found on large reels in the container, Mark secured Louie atop a heavy log as best he could, ensuring he was wrapped up to keep him as warm as possible near the fire. He held a blade over the flames to burn off the oil. He then washed the blade with fresh water before placing it in the fire again. He found a pair of jeweller's needle-nosed pliers which would suffice as tweezers. He sterilised the pliers the same way as the blade.

Try as he might, Mark was unable to hold Louie's toe, the knife, and the glasses at the same time. He required the glasses to see efficiently enough to be able to operate but was unable to secure Louie's toe without needing to hold onto it. Mark decided he would have to jury-rig the glasses into place above the toe with the aid of clamps and angle brackets which he could screw straight onto the log. He was unable to simply place the glasses on his nose as the magnification was too powerful.

Half an hour later Mark had affected the make-shift magnifier suspended above the toe. With sufficient sunlight remaining to see by, Mark set to work. He didn't think Louie was capable of feeling that much as he didn't seem to stir once Mark began a small incision starting from the entrance wound. He used boiled freshwater, now made possible with the discovery of metal pots, to wipe away the blood and putrid pus oozing from the wound. Mark gagged at the stench of it but was able to stop himself from vomiting - just.

He didn't handle the sight of the wound and blood well as he had to cut further into Louie's toe. He worried how deep the object had buried itself. Mark didn't want to cut a gaping hole in the boy's toe which might make matters worse, even without the object in there.

He eventually found the sliver of rusted metal which he could only recognise once he had cleaned it off thoroughly. Once he determined it for what it was, Mark became more concerned than ever. He remembered well his mother's mantra whenever he and his brother stepped on a rusty nail or were cut by corrugated iron; 'up to the doc's for a tetanus booster young man'. He hated the tetanus shots, which, in his young mind, had lagged in his arm forever.

If Louie contracted lockjaw here, there would be nothing he

could do. While he was holding the incision closed with his fingers ready to sew it up with the thin fishing line, he wondered if he should attempt to cauterise the wound rather than suturing. Fire was the great cleanser of all things morbid according to the many Westerns he had enjoyed at the movies.

With the wound cauterised, sutured and bound as best as he was able, Mark wrestled with Louie to untie him from the log before settling him next to the fire. Mark laid behind him adding his warmth to the boy while he fought off the fever and he waited for signs of a break. The late afternoon turned to night and to day again before any sign of improvement was visible.

There was no way for him to know how the symptoms of tetanus presented themselves, nor what he might do should they show, so he was greatly relieved to see improvement. He saw out the fever, swabbing the boy's body and brow during the heat, wrapping himself around the boy during the shivers and hoping like mad that Louie would survive.

Louie finally approached normality on the third day, wearily asking for something to eat. All that was available due to Mark being unable to venture off to forage, was some dried pork, left over from their initial supplies. The other possibility Mark had hoped to find in the container was perhaps canned edibles. Alas, they had to make do with the treasures they did have, rather than wish for what they could not possess.

As Louie improved, Mark was able to leave the boy alone for longer periods. He was able to drop in a line and add a fish or two to their simple diet. Louie's young, healthy body soon flourished under his uncle's care to resemble his former Adonis-like nature, tall and generously muscled for his age. Louie soon felt fit enough to walk without any discernible impairment to his stride and raring to continue with their adventure.

Mark selected a more suitable area up the beach a little, to build a base camp. With the fishing rods and lines at their disposal, and quite a few coconut palms dotting the high water mark, Mark felt sure they would be able to provide for themselves while they laboured. Using bowsaws and axes he was able to make a sturdy shelter capable of accommodating a small cooking/heating fire. A wall to screen off the prevailing winds would keep them warm and dry in most weather conditions other than the foulest storms.

Louie took to fishing with his usual zeal and soon became an excellent provider of fresh fish on a daily basis including a few of the smaller, pesky sharks. A variety of pots and pans from the buried container assisted greatly in keeping sand from their meals. Sand was a constant accompaniment and annoyance to their lives. They had to make sure they washed away all traces of sand from their bodies each and every day to deter the abrasive rashes that resulted from sleeping with the fine grit on their skin.

While Louie tended to the task of provisioning, Mark loaned himself to the difficult task of raft manufacture. They needed a suitable substrate upon which to build their raft. All of Mark's experiments had failed in that regard. While driftwood was plentiful, it lacked the appropriate buoyancy once their weight was added, to effectively carry them for long periods on the water. Once the wood was immersed in water, it became waterlogged and too heavy to keep afloat.

Fastening inflated inner tubes, (achievable using the hand pumps they found), to the logs didn't assist greatly enough to chance the open water. He thought long and hard about the problem with few answers presenting themselves. Mark was swiftly running out of ideas until he saw the half of a coconut that Louie threw in the water, no longer required as water containers, floating off beyond the breakers bound for who knew where. His eyes followed the path of the little vessel until it was well out of sight.

His brain minced over all the possible permutations of his experiments to date without revealing definitive answers. He sat back in the warm sunlight watching Louie cast his fishing line expertly beyond the breakers in the outgoing tide. The shipping container in the foreground, now clearly visible, since the prevailing big tides had washed away the sand surrounding it. It would only take one or more king tides to set the watertight container adrift once more.

Mark even half-heartedly toyed with the idea of floating atop the container out to sea. He threw the idea away as quickly as he had thought it because there was no way to steer the container or to keep it upright once in the swell of the ocean. Something in his mind kept at him, though. Thoughts of the container prickled at his subconscious.

He casually wandered down the beach toward the object that once held such a miraculous cargo. Could there be anything else it might provide he wondered? He mulled over the thought as he man-handled the stiff door open. With a loud creak, the heavy door was pushed aside. Mark inspected the empty container unsure of what he was hoping to see. It was an empty steel container. Nothing but an empty steel…

But it wasn't only steel though was it? It had a floor that was covered. He stared at the smooth plywood surface attempting to dislodge the fug prevented him from grasping the thought, the idea hovering in the back of his mind. Like molasses through a sieve, the notion gradually seeped into his consciousness.

Two days later, the container disappeared. They awoke one morning to find it gone. A squall, coupled with a high tide had moved a sufficient amount of sand to set the container adrift. Mark was grateful that he had not fully fastened the door to return it to its watertight capacity. He didn't like the idea of a floating killer capturing an unsuspecting vessel out at sea. The container would float for a while, then gradually fill with enough water to sink. They had removed the plywood flooring just in time it seemed.

Mark erected a crude gantry with a series of pulleys and ropes with which to lift heavy materials when the time was necessary. Under the gantry, on a series of bracing driftwood logs was the emerging skeleton of what Mark hoped would be a sea-going craft.

The ribs and main beams were fashioned from the softest woods he could find among the stunted trees inland. Hacking a path through the dense bush was made ever so simple with the aid of the machetes and cane knives. The first of the plywood sheets adorned the bow of the vessel secured with glue and screws to the ribs. Getting the correct angle to marry two sheets of ply together on the skeleton proved a tedious task filled with numerous mistakes. Using bevels and squares from their haul made the job possible, but far from easy or perfect.

When the skeleton of the hull was completed nearly a month later, it resembled a squarish version of a small yacht he had once sailed with his brother. It was far from pretty and nowhere near seaworthy until he completed the outer skin of plywood sheeting. Once that difficult task was finished, he concentrated on filling and sealing every joint, hole, and impediment with silicones and putties. He also found a rubber roofing compound among the paint tins, which provided the final waterproofing coat.

Mark lined the inner ribs with polystyrene packing material. He filled the hollow keel with rolls of lead flashing commonly used for lining roof edges to keep the weather out. Mark and Louie scoured the beach for kilometres either side to find a driftwood log of sufficient length and strength to use as a mast. It took many days to return the trimmed log to the camp by rolling it along the beach on smaller logs.

The days and weeks slipped by quickly as they worked all hours to fashion the craft, step the mast supported and secured by galvanised clothesline cable, turnbuckles and galvanised pipe saddles. The work was wearying for two people deprived of the essential vitamins and minerals to keep a person in peak physical condition. Mark explained at length what he planned, showing Louie pictures drawn in the sand of what to expect.

He trained the boy in the basic theory behind sailing so that he would have an understanding of the mechanics involved once they had her afloat. Mark even built a small boat out of a coconut shell similar to the one that gave him the idea, with a sail, to show Louie that his idea was not altogether insane. Louie loved playing with the small boat, marvelling how it glided upon the water with the wind filling its tiny cloth sail.

Mark felt a little glum as he watched Louie playing with what was essentially his first toy. Mark's resentment for the boy's mother, though diminished after his birth, still deprived the boy of the joyous childhood he deserved. He missed out on the genuine affection they could have felt for one another under different circumstances. He wished that he could have had a boy like Louie himself. He promised that if the occasion ever eventuated, he would make amends for the years he had not invested in Louie's happiness.

Sure, Mark had provided for him, given him shelter and surely saved his life on many occasions, but he had never shown the boy the love he should have received from a surrogate parent. Even a Godfather would have shown his Godchild more affection than Mark had displayed. The moment he decided to rescue the infant was the moment he should have cast aside any resentment he felt for the mother, bestowing upon the child a way of life all children deserve.

He could not make up for the lost years, but he was adamant about resurrecting the boy's life by introducing him to civilisation, and yes, his true parent. His biological father had a right to be with his only son, albeit delayed by some years. Mark was desperately determined to give father and son the opportunity that had been denied them. He would sorely miss the boy and hoped he might come to an arrangement with Luke regarding visitation with Louie.

He didn't feel noble at the gesture of uniting the pair, more like, obligated, to do so. As a responsible guardian, he felt compelled to give the boy every opportunity to live a full and normal life with all the comforts. The near call with Louie's infected toe only highlighted the fact that they were in constant danger on the atoll. He owed it to himself and the boy, to do everything in his power to return to Australia before it was too late.

He had seen no passing vessels or planes in the entire time since the crash, only heard one or two at a distance. Mark knew that the only way they could affect a rescue was to get themselves off the atoll under their own steam. The construction of the good ship *Louise* gradually took form, though Louie continued to harbour grave doubts about setting sail. While construction of the main hull had neared completion, the outriggers were still to be built. The lead-filled keel would be inserted, glued and sealed into the hull only once they had transported the vessel to the water-line. It would be impossible to drag or roll the ship with the keel in place. They would need at least twenty-four hours for the silicone and glue to cure once applied, so they had to ensure the tides were right for the launch.

The outriggers would be comprised of two lightweight logs at the end of the struts, with inflated tubes pushed onto them, tied off at both ends. There would be two sets of outriggers giving them fair stability while at sea in most weather conditions. Cheap plastic workman tarps found in the container would be their sails, and while they would not last long in winds of any magnitude, they had ample supplies to replace damaged ones.

Mark had sufficient ropes and pulleys to mimic basic sail manipulation, which comprised a mainsail only. He didn't have the wherewithal to create a jib sail as an accompaniment. He utilised shovels as oars and manufactured oarlocks should the wind abate for any length of time. Everything was of a crude nature without the finesse of a craftsman but should suit the purpose for as long as necessary, or so he hoped.

He allowed Louie his leisure time while he worked at shaping and building outriggers to secure to the ship after rolling the *Louise* down to the water-line. Pipe saddles would secure them to the gunwales fore and aft on starboard and port sides. Long wood screws would fasten the saddles to the internal framework of the boat. The same pipe saddles suitable for securing PVC pipes he used as oarlocks. Mark was rather proud of the crude design of the vessel considering he had next to no building experience other than assembling IKEA furniture. The first shelter he built on the other side of the atoll, at his original camp, was a clumsy, ramshackle affair. His second shelter was almost sophisticated in comparison.

A minimum of a week was required in testing the vessel and their abilities, in and around the atoll before they braved the open water for the first time. Then they would familiarise themselves with open water sailing for a week or two before making the final departure, fully laden with as many provisions as they could conceivably carry. They would be relying heavily on what they might catch on the fishing lines to sustain them on their possibly long, arduous, and dangerous journey.

Mark placed great faith in the *Louise* to remain a seaworthy vessel long enough to enter shipping lanes where they could flag down a ship. There would be the possibility of small cooking fires within the largest pot the container carried, but they were limited in the amount of firewood they could take on board. Their fish would probably have to be eaten raw once their fire supplies ran out. They would leave enough firelighters and leaves with which to signal a ship when they spied one. Water would be a major problem if it didn't rain soon. Their supplies were near an end and Mark had not yet discovered another source during their inland travels.

He planned a pig trap to capture one or two suckling pigs to slaughter for their journey. A simple hole dug in the sand along one of the many trails crisscrossing the inland scrub, covered with a tarp weighed down by stones at the end, sprinkled with sand and leaves, should earn them a reward. Drying the meat as best they could, would require days on the beach with many small, smoky fires surrounding the drying meat. Sufficient hot sunlight to dry the meat was at least one commodity on which they could rely.

Obtaining salt by means of evaporating seawater on garbage can lids would see them being able to salt the pork to a degree.

Many coconuts were gathered to provide nourishment and refreshment should water run out while aboard. A tarp tied together at the four corners would hold the coconuts in place aboard *Louise's* outriggers, and utilised as a drogue, should the need arise.

Several weeks later marked the nine-year milestone of being marooned on the atoll for Mark. Their pig trap had failed to bear fruit so far. Summer storms had come and gone. The *Louise* remained high and dry, awaiting the cooler months before her maiden voyage. Mark hoped to make Australia before Louie's ninth birthday. While life had eased considerably for the pair of castaways, Mark longed for the sights and sounds of civilisation and mature conversation with adult peers. He wanted Louie to experience a proper Christmas and other holidays and festive occasions so lacking in their existence. Most importantly, Louie needed the comradery of other children, not just to play with, but from whom he could learn.

A million little things that he had taken for granted for so long while living his life, had become the focus of his attention once he lost them. Coffee! Oh shit, how he longed for a simple cup of coffee in the morning again. The aroma of the roasted beans percolating in the espresso pot on the stove, one of his favourite things to wake to. Toast with Vegemite, every Australian child's mainstay while growing up. Reading a book, taking a hot shower, hot dogs, beef roasts on a Sunday, dancing, music…and booze. Hmm, a shot of Scotch.

Mark had to stop himself, he was drooling profusely thinking about all the things he missed so badly. The most important things, he convinced himself, were to get the *Louise* sea-worthy. A few months longer and they would be on their way if everything came together as he envisaged.

They would attempt it sooner were the weather cooler, but Mark knew only too well how devastating the high summer temperatures could be. They had run out of sunscreen long ago, so it was best not to tempt fate by choosing the hottest months of the year to be exposed out in the middle of the ocean. As soon as April approached they would drag the boat down the beach for her final fit-out and sea trials. Once they were satisfied that the *Louise* could hold her own on the open ocean, they would set sail.

YEAR TEN

How could things have gone so terribly wrong, Mark wondered as the vessel roared effortlessly over the deep blue ocean swells? The two, one hundred and fifty horse-powered Mercury outboard motors were hardly at full throttle and still, the boat cruised at blinding speed through the near-perfect summer day, slicing through the calm waters of the Pacific with ease. The wind whipped through his long hair tied at the rear with a band. He had shaved off his long beard to reveal a fresh pink face beneath the nine-year growth, but he refrained from cutting off his luxurious locks. He was proud of the fact that he retained hair at all and had not taken after his father or grandfather in that regard - both bald as badgers. Was that even true? Were badgers bald? He didn't think so.

Why, oh why, had they bothered? Why didn't he realise what would happen and simply save them the effort? He knew the answers of course, but couldn't help asking the rhetorical questions just the same. Madness! The whole mess was madness for which he was almost entirely to blame.

The insanity that gripped him after the crash had managed to take hold of him again at the worst possible time, in a method that would never be undone or forgiven. He had made a hash of things, as usual, allowing his baser emotions to rule his rational demeanour. Was he ever rational? He doubted that lately. Seemed rational thought had left the building along with Elvis. Mark seriously doubted he ever had the ability to think rationally given the evidence of his actions once he woke up on that bloody atoll. He wondered if he would ever be capable of it at all.

He questioned every action he had taken, sifted through his motives with a fine-tooth comb without finding evidence that he was ever of sound mind. He sorted through the memories of before the crash and still found very little evidence to the contrary. He began to wonder how he could possibly have seen himself as something other than the monster he had become. He was obviously very clever at deluding himself and others.

He believed everyone felt a certain amount of anger at some time in their lives, shown rage at some point whether justified or not. Surely everyone had moments when they could not control the rage within, lashing out to defend themselves or loved ones? Yet, even as he thought it, Mark knew that normal individuals didn't cross the line as he had done, they stopped short of that boundary between thought and action once they realised the possible ramifications their actions might cause.

He had finally descended to the level of the clients he once represented, had committed the ultimate crime in his mind; murder. He had taken someone's life in a state of premeditated calmness. There was no excuse, no justification for his actions. He would not try to justify his deed by apportioning blame. He knew full-well that he alone had to accept responsibility for everything that occurred from the moment the plane crashed, right up to the time he killed Luke. It was a rolling snowball that simply would not be halted or altered in its path of destruction, an emotional juggernaut bent on murder and mayhem of fully imaginable consequences.

Of course, it was not the only death for which he was being held accountable. No, he had to bear the burden of Louise's death as well as that of her lover. No sooner had they hit the shores of Australia when they were entangled in a major crime intrigue, with him as the main suspect - the 'perp'.

Their story had hit all the major TV and newspaper headlines for weeks following their arrival. Journalists vying for an interview plagued their every waking moment, resorting to any manner of enticement conceivable. Book offers and movie offers poured, money accumulated at an incredible rate while accounts of their survival, true and false, circulated the globe.

Terrorists had come forward after the crash to claim responsibility for the heinous act that saw the demise of the plane, but nobody remembered *them* anymore. No one remembered that a baggage handler and maintenance person planted the bombs. It was all about the miraculous survival of a passenger on that ill-fated flight. The romance of the pre-honeymoon holiday gone wrong.

The whole world cried at the heart-wrenching story of survival against the odds, at the passing of the partner, the heroic effort of the man to rear the infant. All was sunshine and roses for them both until the accusations started rolling in.

Someone had dissected the story to find fault with the glittering tale, to besmirch the episode with onerous tones of incrimination. Someone had so moved the authorities with contradicting versions of the story, that detectives finally interviewed and arrested Mark for the manslaughter of his former fiancée. The detectives interviewed the boy at length to arrive at several possible conclusions, none of which viewed Mark in a favourable light.

Mark had told everyone the absolute truth when asked, without sugar-coating a single portion. His honesty became his ultimate undoing. Mark's feelings of guilt had gnawed at him long enough that he was unwilling to ignore his role in Louise's passing. He admitted to being negligent, and that by so being, had possibly aided her demise. He stopped short of an all-out admission of guilt to the charges, preferring his chances at eluding a jail sentence by defending himself in court.

He didn't think it was possible that a jury of average, law-abiding citizens would convict him. Not when all of Australia had heard of the story, knew of the extenuating circumstances leading up to the evening in question.

Then one bombshell after another descended upon the hapless duo. Louie was immediately taken from him by Child Protective Services. Mark was allowed bail under his own recognisance but refused any contact with Louie. Luke began a heated campaign in the media to ensure the people of Australia knew Louise's side of the story, a very biased portrayal of a woman wronged by a cheating philanderer. No mention was made of the fact that Luke and Louise had been lovers despite Louise remaining in the home she shared with Mark.

It was a dirty vendetta being concocted by a bitter man hell-bent on avenging his lover, creating a trial by media. Mark began to seriously doubt his ability to persuade a jury that he was not the man portrayed so callously by the papers, especially when he felt some of it to be true. He was torn between mixed emotions on that front. What he regretted more than anything was the fact that his first move upon returning to Australian shores was to introduce Louie to his natural father. He could not believe how badly that introduction had concluded.

Once the initial fanfare had subsided to a general tumult, Mark knew that his first act had to be to contact Luke, to formally introduce him to his son. He had every intention of leaving Louie with his father, as it should be. It was the very least he could do for the ill-fated family.

He had prepared Louie for the meeting as best he could, amid awkward explanations of what a father was, and how that father participated in the outcome of Louie's existence. Louie didn't want to either meet or live with his father who was a complete stranger to him. The boy was miserable at the thought of being separated from his beloved uncle, the only father figure he had ever known. The whole experience, from the moment of their rescue, was an overwhelming occasion of confusion and sadness for the boy.

He watched his uncle with undisguised awe as the boat was being built. He could vaguely imagine how the boat resembled his toy coconut boat and that only managed to create grave fears in him for their survival at sea. The hot summer months were drawing to an end and the time of their departure imminent. Louie had faith in his uncle to deliver on his promises, after all, he had built a boat like he said he could.

Whether it would float successfully was yet to be determined, but he had built it using all the strange and wonderful things they found inside the big box. He had no idea that what they discovered could be used to make such wondrous things like their home and the boat. Though he told his uncle that he was prepared to follow his lead, he was dubious about Mark's ability to produce the things he drew in the sand to make Louie understand.

Then Uncle made him the little coconut boat to demonstrate exactly what he had in mind. Louie watched with joy as his little boat sailed out beyond the breakers of their bay on the end of his line, before pulling it back onto the shore.

Still, making the transition from a small toy boat to one in which they might sail away, was a leap of faith too great for Louie to take. He learned more in the short time it had taken to build the boat than in all the time he had been with Uncle. He learned of many strange things such as the names of tools and all the other things they took out of the big box.

He learned to use those tools to make a job much easier than what he was used to. His uncle taught him all about a different kind of life they would experience once they reached Australia. He told Louie about the major cities with buildings so tall they were sometimes in the clouds. That was something that Louie could not imagine or entirely accept as the truth. He had great difficulty accepting much of what his uncle talked about.

Uncle had become a different person altogether. He talked to Louie all the time, even asking his opinion, showing him affection, smiling, laughing, even clowning around and playing with him. Louie could not remember a happier time.

Once he had sampled affection from his idol, Louie craved it more and more. He loved nothing more than spending time in silly games with him on the beach, or wrestling around in the water on those rare occasions when they ventured deeper than ankle depth. Louie's horizons were expanding at a tremendous rate as his uncle filled his young mind with all manner of information that Louie soaked up like a sponge.

The more he learned the more he wanted to know but tried very hard not to ask so many questions that Uncle became angry. Though it seemed that Uncle never got that angry anymore. In the past, he and Mark simply sat around in silence most times, with Mark sporting a menacing frown. Louie always felt as though he had done something wrong, something that irritated his uncle, causing him to resent his presence.

It was a juggling act of conflicting messages where his uncle was concerned. Louie was never quite sure how to read his moods on any given day, or indeed from moment to moment. He always felt as though he had to tread lightly, figuratively and literally, around him. He could be terrifying at times, often shouting and angry. Admittedly, though, Mark had only punished Louie physically a couple of times.

Most times the look on his uncle's face and the deep disappointment in his eyes were enough to deter Louie from ever repeating the infringement, imaginary or otherwise. Louie didn't always know what he had done to gain the disappointment, which made it difficult not to repeat the act. He had grown immensely fond of his role model, looking up to him as only a child might when no comparison was at hand.

He could not understand that there were alternative relationships among humans, as he had never experienced them. To Louie, everyone obviously treated their charges the same way as his Uncle treated him. Only when his uncle changed so dramatically did Louie realise that alternatives existed, that truly remarkable friendships containing joy and laughter were possible.

Louie watched in fascination as Uncle worked on the boat with a singular purpose, ignoring all else whilst doing so. Once finishing a particular section of construction, he then devoted a goodly amount of time to Louie either in lessons or play. The little boat that Mark had made for him filled him with pleasant hours and brought great joy to his heart. He was fascinated by the little contraption, often removing the little triangular sail and mast to visualise the construction better, then reassembling the rigging to a higher degree of efficiency.

He studied how the wind filled the cloth to push the boat away from the shore when it blew in the right direction. He didn't understand how they might steer their boat if the wind didn't happen to be blowing in the right direction for them. Uncle then showed him what he called the tiller, on the boat he was building, explaining how it was used to steer the boat no matter where the wind came from. He explained how it was necessary to tack across the wind in order to gain forward momentum on the right heading.

When Louie thought he understood the purpose of the tiller arrangement and inspected his uncle's construction closely, he set to work to build a similar device for his vessel. Louie didn't understand that human intervention was required to alter course via the tiller aboard a boat. While his little vessel had the rudiments of a tiller similar to the *Louise*, it would not be possible to alter the course once the vessel was afloat.

Louie experimented with tying the tiller at certain angles to steer a certain path, but eventually, he would have to resort to towing the toy back by way of the attached line. Louie looked about him with affection and familiarity. He was saddened greatly at the prospect of leaving his cheerful existence in the only home he had known. He tried to cram as much pleasure as possible from the time that remained, into the hours set aside for playtime.

Gradually the *Louise* took on the shape that Uncle had drawn for him in the sand. The weather cooled and the departure date loomed ominously near. Once the boat was fully assembled at the bottom of the beach, the plan was to sail her around the atoll a few times to measure her seaworthiness and possibly gain a better understanding of the atolls overall dimensions.

After Uncle gauged the *Louise* ready for her sea trials, they would take her out into the rougher open waters surrounding their atoll. Louie would be trained thoroughly in the sailing, the rigging and repairs should they be necessary. He needed to be proficient at all tasks aboard the *Louise* in order to free his uncle for spells while he slept. When all was ready, and Mark deemed the weather sufficiently cooler to attempt the journey, they would load the *Louise* with all the provisions they could pack, all the tools and implements they needed to survive out at sea, as much water as they could safely carry. Everything needed to be strapped down securely. Luckily, some of the packages containing rope had diagrams of different knots that would assist them to secure sails and cargo. Uncle Mark practised them, then passed on that knowledge. Louie soon developed skilful manipulation of the ropes, perfecting the knots with aplomb. Louie loved challenges of mind and body.

Once the *Louise* had entered the water, if she remained afloat, she would have to remain in the water with a long rope securing her to a coconut palm at the top of the beach. From her aft would be a weighted rope to keep her offshore. It would not be convenient to return the boat to shore once the keel was in place, and the outriggers mounted. His uncle hoped that they didn't experience any bad storms before they were ready to depart. If the *Louise* were damaged or destroyed beyond repair they had no hope of building another vessel.

Mark watched the skies apprehensively while he toiled on the boat, explaining to Louie that every screw hole had to be filled with something called silicone, as well as every joint on the outer hull not properly sealed by the bituminous paint. His uncle paid meticulous attention to all the little holes originally drilled to secure the sheets to the floor of the big box. The *Louise* ended up looking like it had spots everywhere. Louie found it difficult to determine if there were more filled up holes than plain plywood sheeting.

Once the final assembly of the *Louise* was completed, keeping one side raised to prevent the keel from digging in, Uncle pushed her into the water until she was floating for the first time. It was a very sunny, calm day with nary a ripple on the surface of the water. Louie didn't think they would be able to sail on a day with no wind, as he had learned with his little boat that he named *Lulu*, after his mother, himself and his mysterious father. Uncle Mark whooped for joy when the *Louise* didn't sink straight away.

His uncle said that the boat was very stable and not leaking at all, that they would wait until later in the day when there was more wind to try her out. Louie dreaded boarding the vessel when he thought about the sharks swimming about underneath them. He often saw sharks inspecting the *Lulu* as it floated beyond the shallows. They pushed it around the surface like they were playing with it, testing the taste occasionally with their mouths.

Mark was extremely relieved at seeing the *Louise* afloat for the first time. Many mistakes had been made and corrected during her construction. Mark had very little experience at building anything other than some model aeroplanes when he was a child. He understood the basics of construction and the rudiments of design but never thought he might need to trust his life to those few experiences.

Louie seemed very reticent as the time grew closer to the launch date. Mark watched him playing more and more with his little *Lulu*, escaping into the activity to keep his mind from the encroaching departure. He understood the boy's reluctance to leave the island, for they had built a home, which they shared amicably. No, he was underplaying the change in their relationship. He and Louie were far more than amicable of late. He had grown an intense affection for the boy. An aching affection leaving him breathless at times. The fact that he had to relinquish all responsibility for Louie to his father once they returned to Australia cut deep to his core, but would not deter him from the path they had begun.

Mark placed an enormous amount of effort into building a boat that he was hoping would survive the enmity of the open ocean. He had read accounts of the *Kontiki* and its epic voyage across a great expanse of the ocean following the path of the ancients. He knew of the perils they faced on that voyage and didn't relish enduring the same tests of courage and ingenuity. His skills were highly debatable when it came to matters of practicality and workmanship. His brain could not be questioned when it came to retaining points of law or precedence, but he failed miserably in most other areas. He was delighted with his efforts to complete a task he had set himself and the boy, overwhelming though it was at the time. The *Louise* floated upon the water easily, without any visible signs of leakage.

The true test would come when the boat was taken to the extremes while fully laden, but for the time being, that it floated was a testament to his determination. It was not a pretty vessel by any stretch of the imagination, but it was possibly their salvation from an eternity marooned on a deserted atoll in the middle of the Pacific. They had to take the chance to leave the atoll, he felt it stronger and stronger with each passing day. A sense of foreboding had taken root at the back of his mind, resilient, onerous, and compelling. He could not ignore the sensation, nor push it from his thoughts, or disguise it with any rational explanation. He was left with no option but to recognise it for what it was and heed its counsel. Such a process was arbitrary to every pattern of behaviour previously known to him, yet Mark was convinced of its accuracy.

The greatest risk to the vessel were the few weeks it would be moored each night. It was totally necessary to test the *Louise* first before making way. It was also imperative to school himself and Louie in her operation. Although Mark had sailed as a youngster he was far from proficient. He would require as much schooling and practise as Louie. He would not fall victim to overconfidence or appear a total know-all in front of the boy. He would make his mistakes as they learned, and take his rebukes as they came. He was, if anything, his hardest taskmaster.

He had taken it upon himself to teach Louie as much as he possibly could about everything he had neglected over the previous years. His complacency in that regard stemmed from the deep abiding resentment he harboured toward the boy's mother. Once Mark broke through the emotional barrier which had served to limit his involvement with Louie, their relationship soared, and Mark was finally comfortable when dealing with him.

He realised that taking responsibility for raising a child encompassed far more than taking care of physical needs. The educational and emotional elements of child-rearing were equal, if not more important. His neglect of Louie's education may well have retarded the boy's ability to learn in the future. The developmental years were crucial in the structure of a human being's mental and physical growth. Louie's emotional development through nurture and love was severely lacking, thanks to Mark's inability to see through the hostile barrier he had erected around himself.

Mark completely wasted the first eight years of the boy's life, which was unforgivable. He promised himself and the boy's mother and father, to make amends. His first order of priority was to secure a physical future for Louie. That meant returning to Australia. Until they attained that goal, it was Mark's intention to drill the boy in the basics.

A simple box the size of a computer screen containing moist sand, with a stylus made of a sharpened stick, was all that was required to begin teaching Louie the alphabet, and the beginning of simple sums. Louie could read tracks in the sand to recognise immediately the animal that made them but had no understanding of letters or numbers in the written form. Thankfully, Mark had a good grasp of the English language, which meant that Louie had a reasonable vocabulary, albeit spiced with quite a few swear words!

Lessons started early in the morning and in the evening for a duration of one and a half hours per session. Mark soon found that Louie was a quick learner with a keen intellect. He soaked up the knowledge imparted to him with an eagerness that thrilled Mark. He was impressed when he found Louie practising writing his alphabet outside lessons, sitting alone on the beach with his tongue poking from the side of his mouth in intense concentration. Mark didn't place much faith in his abilities as a teacher, so finding the boy able to grasp the concepts of the written language so readily made him sigh with relief.

He had no hopes of seeing Louie up to the standard required for a pupil of his age group, but he felt confident that Louie would at least be literate. Mark made a little competition for the boy once he knew his alphabet and some basic words and sentences. He would scribe a sentence or two at the low water mark as the tide was coming in, giving Louie only a short time in which to read the inscription before it was erased by the incoming tide.

Louie's passion for learning became evident when he cursed himself for not being able to translate the message in time. He worked harder and harder until he became proficient enough to read and understand the inscription every time, regardless of its length. One particular message made the boy smile with great enthusiasm. It read, 'Louie is a good boy'.

Whenever Mark praised the boy he would throw himself into Mark's arms almost shivering with appreciation. Mark had trouble sometimes remembering that Louie, despite his advanced physical attributes, was after all, still a child. An impressionable child, willing to take on board most of what life threw at him with a clear head, and a soft heart. Mark was sometimes surprised by the look of pure adoration in Louie's eyes during the time they spent together.

The day came when all the trials were completed, when the *Louise* had stood up to the tests of the sea and the wind with flying colours, and Louie was as proficient in the act of sailing her as his uncle. Mark had earmarked the following morning with an outgoing tide as their ideal departure date. They had loaded all the provisions aboard the vessel during the afternoon, including the dried meat of the pig, they managed to catch a week prior.

With victualling complete, they would shove off at first light keeping the rising sun on their left, heading due south, in the hope that they were heading in the right direction. After all, Australia had to be south of their position. Louie was particularly glum and morose, shuffling about, scuffing the sand in a petulant manner. Mark didn't try to persuade Louie that he should not feel sad. He understood what it meant to leave home for the first time. When a younger Mark had made the decision to leave his home, he had been excited, yet very sad at the same time. Mark simply placed a comforting arm around Louie's shoulder when they both sat down next to their campfire.

That evening they talked quietly to each other about all their concerns, hopes, and wishes. Mark minced no words when it came to letting Louie know about returning him to his father. There was simply no way around that fact. Louie and he were to be separated once they reached Australian shores. No matter how hard Louie tried to dissuade his uncle from that course of action, Mark stood firm.

"Louie, you have to understand, mate. Luke is your natural father, and once he knows his son is alive and well, he'll want to have you with him, as any father would. I'll miss you like hell, mate but it is not negotiable. It's one of the big reasons we're leaving here, to reunite you with your father. If I was your father I would want to have you with me very much, and it wouldn't matter who looked after you until that time, I would still want you with me. You have to accept that, Louie. I'll ask, Luke if he'll allow me to visit with you, and all we can hope is that he'll say yes. We'll find a way of compromising with everyone including the authorities. I have no legal rights to your guardianship, Louie. Luke is your father and I have to respect the law.'

"Why don't we just stay here then, Uncle?"

"Aww, Louie, we'll die here way before our time I reckon. Sooner or later something'll happen that we can't fix ourselves. I'm pretty much okay with it for myself, but I can't let that happen to you, mate. You deserve a chance to live a full life, to meet other kids and to develop relationships with girls, to live and grow to your full potential. I can't give you that here. We are never going to be rescued from this bloody place, so it's up to me to get us back. It's going to be dangerous out there I know, but we have to take the chance, buddy. We got really lucky finding all the stuff to help us, but it would not be enough to help us in a medical emergency. You're young and you have a lot of mischiefs to get up to yet, lots of accidents to survive as part of that growing experience. I would never forgive myself if something like that happened before you had a chance to experience another way of life.'

"I understand, Uncle but I'm really sad. I don't want to be with someone I don't know, even if he is this father to me you keep talking about. What does it mean anyway? You said the woman called, Louise was my mother and that you cut me out of her belly. What has this other man got to do with it?"

"Oh brother, you really going to hit me with the age-old question right now? Oh, Louie, I don't know if I can explain that properly just now. Hell! I guess you need to know something otherwise, it just doesn't make sense, does it? Okay, okay…shit. Human beings and most other animal species on earth have two genders, male and female. You and me, we are males, Louie. Your mother, she was a female. It takes both genders to produce a baby naturally, mate. When a male and female join to make love, have sex, it's possible for the male to impregnate the female. That means a baby starting inside the female's womb. Nine months later the baby, most times, is ready to come out of the female naturally, head first. You, on the other hand, decided you wanted to stay inside by curling up on your side and refused to face the world. If I didn't cut you out of your mother, both of you would have died. Luke was the male who impregnated your mother even though Louise and I were going to be married."

"I wish you had imp…impreg…ated my mother. Then you would be my father and we could live together."

"Im-preg-nated. It should have been that way, Louie, it really should have, and I want exactly the same thing with all my heart. It was the reason I was so angry with your mother for so long, mate. We were supposed to be married and have children and all that. We were on our way to having a holiday before we actually got married, but your mum didn't want me anymore and told me she was pregnant with another man. I didn't cope with that news well, Louie. It broke me up inside, twisted my guts into a million knots. I came apart, Louie and I acted badly, to myself and her. I was the reason she was alone in that shack, dying while giving birth to you. I have no excuse for my mean behaviour. You should really be glad to be rid of me, I'm not a good person.'

"But my mother was bad first, Uncle. You should have been very angry with her. What she did was not very nice."

"That may be, Louie but it doesn't excuse my behaviour. I don't say that I should have forgiven her and forgotten everything, but I shouldn't have driven her off and hurt her. No human should ever do that to another human no matter how they feel. Anger never solves a problem, Louie, remember that. Anger, resentment, and jealousy are the precursors to war between friends, lovers, neighbours and nations. The anger of many megalomaniacs led to entire nations being duped into bigotry and intolerance, leading to the biggest wars the modern world has seen. No, Louie, I was wrong to act the way I did. I'm deeply ashamed of those actions, which is why I broke down and cried when I saw your mother's grave. I once loved that woman despite any problems our relationship had at the time. Don't feel bad about leaving me, mate, I deserve it and you deserve better.'

"I will never love another person like I do you, Uncle. I never want to be with anyone else."

"I'm flattered, Louie, and believe me, I feel the same, but someday you'll meet a pretty young girl and your heart will melt. If she is truly the one for you, you'll leave me in a heartbeat. You'll want nothing more than to spend every waking moment with her until the day you die. That is the opportunity I want to give you.

Without that experience, without ever making love, you will not truly have lived at all. No one deserves to be deprived of that essential element of life. To have only myself in your life would be a cruel travesty. Please be happy with my decision, Louie, it's all I can give you, my greatest gift, that you get to live a life if we make it out of here and back to Australia.'

"Will we make it?"

"If this weather starts to pick up, we may find out sooner than we want. Don't like the feel of that wind at all, Louie. No, I can't guarantee we'll make it. I can only do my best to at least give it a shot."

Mark's prophetic words proved correct towards midnight. A howling wind woke them from their light sleep. Mark had to douse the fire with sand before the wind had a chance to whip it up. If the fire blew out of control the whole atoll might be set ablaze.

No sooner had the thought entered his mind when the building storm blew a gust that destroyed the walls of the shelter in one go. Luckily Mark managed to kill the flames before they could spread. The roof of their shelter soon followed the wall as the storm's intensity increased. Lightning struck and thunder filled the heavens with a gigantic show of light and sound. Mark raced down to the beach to see to the safety of their boat, while Louie was left to secure the remains of the camp as best he could.

Mark's worst fears were realised when he saw the maelstrom tossing their boat about as easily as Louie's toy. The mooring line was pulled taut as a bowstring and their vessel was in danger of breaking free. To take the risk of leaving the atoll during the middle of a treacherous storm weighed heavily on Mark's mind, while to allow the boat and all their efforts to be ruined seemed equally absurd.

Mark looked up the beach in time to see Louie struggling to remain grounded. He yelled at the boy to make his way down the beach. Although Louie was unable to hear him above the raging roar of the winds, he did make out the hand signals for him to join his uncle. The nylon rope holding the boat from being swept out to sea snapped suddenly, leaving Mark barely holding on with enough strength to keep the boat from disappearing.

Louie fought the idea of boarding the boat during a major storm but feared the alternative when he witnessed the demise of their camp and everything in it. Their home had been completely destroyed in the blink of an eye, and had they stayed at camp protecting it, they might have perished. Mark didn't wait for Louie to make a decision. He seized the boy under the armpits and flung him with all his might into the boat, then quickly grabbed the trailing end of the rope, to be dragged inexorably behind the fleeing vessel.

After Louie untied the remaining anchor line, the boat quickly floated out beyond the breakers into a swell, the like of which neither Mark nor the boy had ever witnessed. Mark was still being towed behind the boat as it jetted out to sea of its own accord, pushed by the fierce winds and tide. The gutters and peaks of the enormous swells seemed impossible to Mark's eyes as he trailed the boat some ten metres or more. He could make no headway along the rope. It was all he could do to keep a hold of the rope which he managed to eventually secure around him. He sputtered and gagged as the saltwater threatened to force its way down his throat while he desperately gasped for air.

Louie tied himself securely to the boat as he had been instructed many times. He could not pull Mark in on the bowline, he simply lacked the strength to do so. Whitewater crashed all about him as the frothy soup swaddled the boat at the crest of each wave. The bag of coconuts atop the outriggers ripped free, plunging into the water behind the boat. Its rope attached to the *Louise* held fast for the time being. Its purpose as a drogue, slowed the boat sufficiently to eventually allow Mark to haul himself forward. He clambered aboard the *Louise* at long last in a breathless, exhausted heap.

His muscles had turned to rubber with the exertion required of the mammoth effort. He could barely raise an arm to place around Louie. The storm continued to toss them about like confetti in the wind for hour after hour, all through the long dark hours of the morning. Pure mental and physical exhaustion gripped the hapless adventurers as they clung for dear life to the swamped boat and each other.

Were it not for the extreme buoyancy of the outriggers and the polystyrene stuffed into the interior of the boat, they would have foundered at the start. Had Mark's design been flawed to a greater extent, it would have cost them their lives before the journey had begun.

They were not out of the woods by a long shot but felt somewhat assured by the fact that the vessel remained afloat. They both bailed out the water as quickly as they could with pots and pans, only to have the boat filled with the following wave. Still, they persisted to bail despite the seeming futility of the gesture. The swells rose to impossible heights, sending them towards the bottoms of the gutters with frightening speed. Were it not for the drogue that miraculously remained attached to the boat, they would have been plunged into the very depths of the gutters from which there would be no return.

Each time the boat threatened to slam into the water far below, they came up short by the sea anchor, allowing them to drift up and over the next swell. The horizontal rain battered them from all sides it seemed, aided by the salt spray whipped by the deafening winds. Mark supposed that they were caught smack in the middle of a hurricane. Knowing that didn't help them one whit.

For two long days, Mark and Louie were assaulted by the heavy seas despite the worst of the hurricane passing. They were unable to eat, drink or sleep enough to create any comfort. Louie copped the worst of it as seasickness wracked his thin body with convulsive heaving that wrought nothing from within his weakened stomach.

The boy had turned a shade of green that caused Mark great

anxiety. He urged the boy to take a mouthful of anything just so he had something in his gut to throw up. Gradually the boy grew weaker and weaker until he feared he had lost him. Mark tilted the boy's head up as he cradled him in his arms, sick and spittle dribbling from his mouth.

Mark washed away the detritus and forced a swallow of water down his throat. The boy was suffering acute dehydration as a result of vomiting every few seconds. The rain had ceased, but the high winds continued to whip them from stem to stern.

Finally, on the third day, the wind abated, the sea calmed and the travellers fell into unconscious sleep. Their battered bodies could take no more punishment, they were incapable of lifting another potful of water out of the boat. They were exhausted beyond human endurance, their muscles wasted and their minds numbed with fatigue.

The calming sea rocked them gently as they drifted to who knew where and didn't care. Neither of them dreamed a single dream or thought a thought as they slept the sleep of the dead. They were incapable of arousing themselves until they were allowed to recoup. They slept for twenty-four hours straight.

When Mark finally awoke on the fourth day at sea, his limbs felt like lead, his head felt like it weighed a tonne with an enormous hammer slamming against the side of it. He managed to right himself sitting waist-deep in water. The boat foundered precariously, weighed down with water. The outriggers threatened to break away from their mounts as they struggled to keep the vessel afloat.

Despite his battered body being abused to within an inch of its life, Mark began to bail out the water using the very last of his strength. Louie stirred from his slumber, still too weak to be of any assistance. Mark assured him he was capable of bailing out by himself, that the boy should rest, conserve his strength. He urged the boy to eat and drink something to replenish what he had lost. Louie sat hunched in the bow miserably chewing on some dried but soaked pork.

"Are we there yet?"

Mark looked at Louie in absolute astonishment, then broke into wild laughter that assaulted his weakened body. When Louie looked at him questioningly, he laughed even harder, causing Louie to smile, then laugh himself. They released all the pent up anxiety and fear of the last few days in a riotous display of mirth. Louie laughed long and hard despite not knowing the reason, he just continued to laugh each time his uncle started. They spurred each other on until they ran out of breath, glad to be alive, glad to be sharing the adventure, glad of each other's company.

They relaxed into an amiable silence with an occasional giggle erupting in turn. Mark was able to empty the boat of its excess water, then turned his attention to providing a proper hot meal. With the wind no more than a slight breeze, he thought they could risk a small fire with which to heat a broth of fish should they be able to catch one. However, dry wood for a fire proved an impossibility.

Catching fish didn't cause concern for the two or more weeks they sailed the ocean without a single clue as to their whereabouts. Mark had no idea how to navigate by stars other than some vague notion about the Southern Cross and had only the idea of keeping the rising sun on his left during the morning and setting sun on the right. They were probably sailing in circles for all he knew. The *Louise* had come through the hurricane essentially intact. A small manageable leak had sprung up in the bow of the vessel, no doubt from smashing into wave after wave during that perilous engagement with nature. Their water reserves were diminishing quickly without the benefit of the backup coconut supply which eventually snapped free during the roller-coaster ride. It had probably saved their lives, though, so all was forgiven.

Louie came alive despite the monotony of endless days upon an open ocean. He had spied whales, dolphins, and huge sharks. Cuttlefish and squid amused him no end, as did the flying fish erupting all about them at times when chased by predators.

He praised Mark to the skies for engineering such a marvel as the *Louise*, to withstand such weather as they had experienced. He thought surely that his uncle was a veritable genius. Mark mused at how much of a genius he might be when he knew nothing of navigation. They might well perish out in the middle of the ocean far sooner than on the atoll they left. He did wonder, though, about how the atoll had fared through the storm.

Of the camp, there would be nothing left. Of that, Mark was certain. All the hardware items they had found were wrapped in poly tarps and buried under the sand. Mark was not sure why he took the time to do that. Perhaps, if anyone else ever ended up there, it might help them to survive. He had inscribed a message on a piece of driftwood above the burial site to explain the contents of the treasure below. There were many useful items to someone finding themselves marooned there. He hoped it might make a difference someday.

Mark scanned the horizon morning, noon, and evening without sighting a single sign of rescue. Whether he had managed to navigate to a shipping lane, under a flight path, or what, he couldn't begin to know. He hoped it would not be much longer, or that they didn't have to face any more frightening storms. He'd had his fill of adventure and excitement for one lifetime.

He wanted to get home, write a book, sell his story and reap the rewards as he kicked back in style. He had no doubt whatsoever that their story was worth a bundle. He would ensure that a trust was set up for Louie's share which he would enjoy when he came of age. A nest-egg sitting safely in the bank for ten years or more should see Louie and his father comfortable for life. He longed for the day when he could finally unite the father with his long-lost son whom he could not know existed.

A trawler saw the smoke signal almost a week later as the last of their water had been consumed. Mark peered at the horizon through bleary eyes already hurting from the early morning glare.

When he spied the odd shape breaking the clean line of the horizon, Mark startled Louie with his urgency.

They quickly started a fire in the empty water container, a galvanised garbage bin. He threw on the leaves they had been carrying in the event of a sighting, igniting them with the firelighters salvaged from the shipping container. It produced a billowing cloud in the clear calm skies, perfect for a distress signal. He used a tarp to interrupt the smoke to produce what he hoped would be recognised as a smoke signal. A constant stream of smoke may be mistaken as simply a fire upon an atoll or the like, whereas a broken stream would indicate intervention. Mark didn't believe in religion or deities of any description, but he wished with all his might that the signal would be seen.

It was. An American trawler working out of the Marshall Islands spied the smoke almost immediately but was unable to haul in its nets while it was on a good run. The captain kept a close eye on the vessel through his binoculars as they hunted their prize. He plotted their approximate position on his G.P.S. though, just to be safe.

It would be several hours before they were able to reverse their direction. The captain, Edward Short, radioed in the sighting in the hope that another vessel may be closer than he but was informed that he was the only vessel thereabouts. Captain Short was dubious about rendering assistance if the boat turned out to be refugees from some war-torn country. Many countries around the world were struggling to know how to handle the refugee situation. The numbers were increasing around the globe as shonky traders ripped off innocents to take them across the oceans in unseaworthy vessels not fit for human habitation.

The swarthy trawler captain didn't want to become ensnarled in a mid-sea brawl with a bunch of non-English speaking, bedraggled and confused victims of nefarious scams.

Something about the vessel seemed odd, though. Smoke from the boat floated aloft in intermittent puffs, indicating desperation of sorts. Usually, boat people were reluctant to draw attention to themselves unless they were foundering. If the vessel were on fire, a continuous stream of billowing smoke would be visible. The boat he saw at a vast distance showed no signs of such distress.

The odd, crude sail and structure of the boat didn't seem congruent with the usual assortment of the derelict death traps floating upon the dangerous seas. The captain fired his flare gun to communicate to the boat that he had seen them. To convey his intentions of performing a rescue at his earliest convenience. Halfway through his run he lost sight of the boat but knew he could find it again easily enough.

Mark screamed for joy when he spied the flare slowly arcing above the horizon. The ship had seen them, they would be rescued at long last. Then the ship slipped from sight, leaving him doubtful. Mark explained to Louie carefully what he thought might be happening. That maybe the boat had something to do first. What that was, though, Mark had no idea, but he knew the boat had seen their smoke, the flare proved it. Of course, there was always the possibility that the boat would not rescue them, that they were on the wrong side of the law perhaps. If that were true they would not have shot off the flare surely? They would simply have ignored their plight.

The thought that they might be finishing a trawling run didn't strike Mark until the ship eventually came into view clearly, with outriggers extended on either side from which to stabilise their vessel. Louie smiled uncertainly, while Mark sighed with relief that a great burden had been raised from his shoulders. He had delivered on his promise to see the boy be given a chance at life off the atoll. He found himself relaxing for perhaps the first time in many months, if not years. Their dreams were answered.

Far from having dreams come true, the nightmare began the moment he returned to Australia. Newspaper accounts of their story and subsequent rescue carried to all parts of the globe before their triumphant arrival on Australian shores. Once the brouhaha simmered down to a mere melee, unrest became apparent regarding the fatality of Louise Campbell.

An emotional storm was being stirred up to a fever pitch from an unknown quarter about the wrongful death quoted in the stories of Mark and Louie's survival. Someone was championing the cause to see justice done. Mark and Louie were separated a mere week after they landed at Tullamarine Airport in Melbourne, Australia. Child Protective Services took charge of Louie, while the police escorted Mark to the nearest station for questioning. It soon became very obvious to Mark that he might be facing a court trial and a possible jail sentence.

At first, it didn't seem that the police were all that interested in prosecuting Mark, but gradually they were swayed when Mark's full, honest confession confirmed the accusations being levelled at him. Mark's hand was the hand that held the implement that severed the victim's flesh.

They believed they could get a jury to convict on the simple facts. Mark believed he could sway a jury otherwise once they were aware of *all* the facts. What became Mark's Achilles' heel was the sworn statement in which he confessed to feelings of hatred toward Louise, and the assault on her with rocks.

Mark gave them all the ammunition they needed without resorting to lawyerly tactics. He didn't want to play those games anymore. He didn't want to besmirch Louise's name or that of her son, by lying or withholding information to defend himself.

Mark's image transmuted from hero to villain overnight in the media. The public demanded a swift justice, tried and found guilty in the press long before a court date. Accounts of Mark's former questionable clients and their exploits once acquitted, circulated among the headlines.

Quotes from former colleagues and prosecutors damned Mark for defending the trash of Melbourne. Everyone seemed eager to jump on the bandwagon, to gain *their* moment of notoriety in front of the camera, or on the page of a newspaper. Only Mark's sister, mother, and father rallied to his defence amid a storm of vitriol, condemning him, forcing him to lower his head in shame.

Staying with his sister, Mark worked hard at preparing himself for the trial. He also managed to slip away now and again to attend to certain other preparations. He was denied any physical contact with Louie, nor would any written communication be allowed. That fact was eating Mark up inside, making him an insomniac, unable to eat as much as he should and often throwing that up.

He feared greatly for Louie's happiness knowing that the media circus must be distressing for the lad. He hoped Louie would not resort to lies in order to help him. He hoped the boy would simply tell the whole truth as he knew it. Mark held nothing back when he finally told the lad everything, so he hoped Louie would do the same no matter how damning it sounded.

When he finally found out that Luke was the kingpin behind all of the public outcry, he could not quite believe it. He was never convinced that Luke loved Louise, of that he felt certain but he didn't figure on such devotion producing the enmity he displayed. Mark knew Luke from way back.

They had both attended the same primary school in a small rural town for one year while Luke's mum taught there. He was a little strange even back then if Mark remembered it correctly. Luke would always be lingering around the showers feigning great camaraderie with all the boys despite not being regarded all that well. It seemed Luke was always hanging around him as well. Turn around and there he was, smiling, wanting to talk, ready to take Mark's side in any squabble.

Mark ran into Luke after moving to Melbourne to take up his studies. He accepted an invitation to go for a drink in the city with Luke, though he really wasn't looking forward to it. He recalled how uncomfortable he felt in the gay bar Luke recommended. Luke seemed to know most of the other patrons who all had a word or two to say as they passed their table.

Mark used a phone trick, arranging for his sister to call him at a certain time. Mark used it to get out of another round of drinks and more inane conversation about nothing, or rather it was nothing to Mark. Luke seemed to revel in the whole camp, double *entendré* in every sentence thing. He swore that Luke had even developed a lisp. Mark couldn't get out of there, away from Luke, and the whole scene, fast enough.

If Luke and Louise were definitely having an affair, which he didn't think Louise would lie about, he knew there was no love there on Luke's side. He had seen Luke at a distance a few times after that day in the bar and it was always with men, arm in arm and even openly kissing one time in Brunswick Street. When Luke spotted him, Mark darted away quickly into traffic, hopping onto a tram to avoid contact.

Mark could not work out why Luke harboured such hostility toward him. It seemed falsely exaggerated to Mark's way of thinking. If, in fact, he did like Louise enough to 'change teams', as it were, it didn't strike Mark as enough to warrant the tide of rage attached to the incriminations. Something was amiss but didn't come to light in Mark's mind.

While the nightmare unfolded for month after month, Mark brokered book deals and movie rights to assist with his legal costs and living expenses. Needless to say, he could not return to work as a lawyer with a trial pending and so fell into the only avenue open to him; exploiting his situation, which didn't overly upset his sensibilities. Mark made sure that every cent was accounted for in his dealings and that clear contracts naming Louie as an equal partner were executed. Bank accounts were set up in both their names and money was divided equally.

Mark didn't have to pay rent to his sister Brianna but managed to pay his way in food and utilities. Brianna made only a modest income as an actress when spreading a few month's work over a year of semi-employment. The trial and fending off reporters accounted for ninety per cent of Mark's available time, with the remaining ten per cent dedicated to his extra projects. He was out on bail and therefore maintained constant communications with the police. His expired passport had long been lost due to the crash, so he had nothing to surrender to the police in that regard.

Luke was a force to be reckoned with when it came to trial by media. Not a day went by when Mark didn't see some story or new accusation levelled at him by way of Luke's obvious testimony. The vendetta aimed at Mark was a relentless obsession by the boy's father to exact revenge for Louise's death.

One reported accusation had Mark nearly choking on his breakfast toast one morning as he scanned the papers. In the latest round of Mark's alleged atrocities was the ridiculous suggestion that he and Louie had *eaten* Louise to stay alive. The newspapers were running with each and every ludicrous comment Luke uttered for the sheer sensation it caused. Mark refrained from answering any questions from the hundreds of phone calls and reporters camped outside his sister's flat. He ignored them totally, a nearly impossible task at times.

Despite the public outrage toward him, Mark still felt a modicum of confidence that he would be able to avoid a sentence over the allegations. He believed his chances to be about fifty-fifty either way. He was by no means certain and planned accordingly, to ensure Louie's welfare if the worst should happen. He knew that the police were not eager to present the case, but had little choice, in the light of the pressure forced on them by the growing media sentiment spurred on by Luke.

As time marched by, Mark detected that the reports in the media were dwindling in frequency and exaggeration. His stories no longer warranted front-page headlines, being relegated more and more toward the end of the papers. Luke's impetus was waning and his rhetoric was gaining much less notoriety and support. Be that as it may, it still beggared belief when Luke turned up at Brianna's front door.

"Has something happened to, Louie, is he alright?"

"We'll get to that. I want to talk to you."

"I'm not allowed to have any contact with you, so you better f…get going."

Before Mark fully realised what was happening, Luke produced a knife from somewhere which he plunged into Mark's abdomen while pushing him inside the unit with his other hand firmly on Mark's chest. No reporters, usually to be found camped outside the unit, appeared to be lurking at that time, so there were no witnesses. Brianna had left for a round of auditions in the city which gave Luke the perfect opportunity to extract his pound of flesh.

He pushed Mark roughly into the unit, closing the front door behind him. Mark staggered backwards to the living room where he collapsed onto a sofa, clutching his side where the knife had penetrated. Thankfully Luke's aim was off by just a few millimetres and no vital organs or arteries had been severed, yet copious amounts of blood oozed from the wound. Mark staunched the flow of blood as best he was able while his befuddled mind tried to take in what was happening.

"You're not gonna get away with it you bastard. I'm gonna make sure of that. You murdered Louise and now you think you can get away with it because you are some hot-shot fucking lawyer? No fucking way, cunt. It ends here, now. You're gonna pay. An eye for a fucking eye, you're gonna pay, arsehole."

"You're mad."

"No shit, Sherlock? Course I'm fucking mad. I'm mad as fucking hell that everyone thinks you're gonna get off, that you're good enough to talk your way out of paying for your fucking crime. Well, it's not getting to court, shithead. I'm ending it. You have been found guilty and you're gonna pay big time."

"For fuck's sake, why, Luke? What did I ever do to you to make you hate me so much?"

"Don't play games with me, you're not gonna talk yourself out of it with me, you piece of shit. You know damn well what you did to me and you're gonna get everything that's comin' to you."

Mark was in pain and not thinking very clearly, but had absolutely no idea what Luke was blathering about. The blood flow seemed to have temporarily abated, but Luke still had the razor-sharp knife in his hand ready to inflict more pain at any moment. All Mark could think of was to keep Luke talking as long as possible, wait for an opportunity to present itself. Nothing the man said made any sense. He could think of nothing that he had done directly or indirectly for Luke to respond with such insane ferocity. One thing Mark was good at, though, was his job back in the day. He hoped he could summon up some of the old courtroom nous he once displayed with alacrity.

"Okay, I understand that you're totally pissed off with me, Luke, I get it. I am sorry that I don't remember the reason why you feel that way, that somehow I caused this intense animosity. Could you just calm down a little and tell me what it was? First, though, can you just tell me if Louie is okay?"

"Fuck Louie. This is about you and me, and you'll never get your hands on Louie, I made sure of that."

Mark felt a leaden dread descending upon him with those words. Spittle flew from the corners of Luke's mouth each time he uttered a word. The pure hatred emanating from every pore made Mark remember the same feelings he had experienced while marooned. He didn't like where the conversation was heading and feared for Louie's life. Luke was granted custody of the boy the moment Mark informed the authorities of Louise's confession. As Louie's sole parent, Luke could keep Mark away from him as long as he liked.

What Mark couldn't understand is why Luke would harm his own child. He wanted to question Luke further on Louie's health but knew he couldn't push the subject. The man had another agenda on his mind, and Mark needed to pursue that line of thought from Luke. He desperately needed to keep him talking about something he obviously wanted to speak about rather than anger him further. Luke sat opposite Mark in a lounge chair with the bloody knife clutched in his hand resting on the arm of the chair.

Luke trembled with incoherent rage as he watched Mark struggle to come to terms with the possibility that he had harmed Louie. He smiled gleefully at the recognition of his adversary's physical and mental anguish. Everything he had planned was slowly coming to fruition. He would reveal his intentions and confess all at last.

After nearly a decade of uncertainty, never knowing if Mark or Louise had survived the plane crash, he was finally able to see the culmination of all his plans clearly coming to fruition. Admittedly, he had to improvise a lot along the way. Killing Mark was never his intention, causing untold emotional agony would have sufficed. Unfortunately, his campaign in the newspapers had run its course. They were no longer interested in what he had to say, even casting grave doubts on his allegations.

What pissed him off, though, what pissed him off more than anything else, was the fact that the arrogant prick didn't actually remember, didn't know! Typical of the conceited bastard that he would not deign to remember something of such importance to someone else. Self-centred cunt was always like that. Always so cock-sure of himself, confident of every move he made. God's gift to the fucking world.

Well, he'd see. He would make sure the bastard saw everything and paid for it. He had all the time in the world to administer all kinds of torment to the helpless bastard. He would inflict the tortures of hell upon Mark, but first, Luke had to calm down, to gather himself and not let his rage get out of control too soon. That time would come and he would unleash the madness of the universe upon him. Until then he needed the prick to know why, and what he had done.

"You really don't know what you did?"

"Not a fucking clue."

"Well, that makes sense coming from a prick like you. Why

would you remember? Why would you give a fuck what you did to someone?"

"I haven't *done* anything to anyone, Luke, least of all you. I hardly know you, or even really knew you, even after spending, what was it, a year, in the same primary school? I haven't known you well enough or long enough to have *done* a fucking thing to you."

Luke lunged at Mark with pure animal rage plunging the knife into his thigh, screaming in a madman's surreal, nightmarish fervour. Luke withdrew the knife and himself out of Mark's reach before he was able to react in any way other than yell in pain and clutch his new wound. Mark was stunned by the ferocity shown by Luke, crippled by the searing pain in his side and his leg. He was unable to string two coherent thoughts together to conclude the madman's intentions or the cause.

Mark had told the truth which only inflamed Luke more. Mark didn't know the cause of Luke's animosity, could not guess at any perceived act which would drive Luke to this demented state. He recognised the driving symptoms of lunacy, though. Mark had first-hand knowledge of the path to irrational rage. He saw the same patterns emerging in Luke's behaviour. If he were not more careful he would not survive the day. Luke was entirely blinded by revenge of some sort. Mark saw his duty as one of a listener, to draw out the tale rather than antagonise the storyteller. He would have to be extremely cautious.

"Luke, just please tell me what it is I've done. I honestly don't know."

"Course you don't, you arrogant turd. People like you have no feelings or concerns for others, too interested in your own shitty lives. Think you're better than *us*, off to university to study law, forgetting all about those you trampled on along the way. Yeah, one year we were together in primary school. One year that changed my life. It should have changed yours too. Should have made you see what I saw, what I discovered about us."

"What? What did you discover, Luke, tell me?"

"*Us*, I discovered *us*."

"Us?"

"You and me. I discovered that we were the same, wanted the same things."

"I still don't…"

"*Us,* arsehole, *us*! Are you listening to me? Do I have to make *sure* you're listening again?"

"No, no, Luke you don't have to do that. Please, I'm trying to find out what you mean. I don't understand what you're trying to tell me. Explain how it happened, how you found out about…us."

"You should *know*, bastard. I shouldn't have to explain anything, that's what this is all about. You're making me very angry."

"I'm sorry, Luke, I really am. If I don't remember then I simply don't remember and if that is making you angry, then all I can say is I'm sorry. If you start explaining it all to me then you might jog my memory. If it is important to you that I remember, then you have to explain it, Luke. You're right I'm a dumb bastard for not knowing, I know that. I wish I could, I really wish it."

"Grovelling doesn't sit well with you, does it? How does it feel to be the one asking to be recognised now, huh? How does it feel to be part of the downtrodden for once? Ugly, isn't it? Well, I had to live that way for years after, *us*. Hurting deeply inside from the rejection while you just flounced around as if nothing happened. You have to *remember,* you pathetic cunt! You have to *remember* the day we were in the shower together, after sports class? You just have to remember that you let me…you know, hold you?"

"You can't be serious? That, that's what all this is about? I let you touch my cock for a moment in the shower while we were in primary school together? A little bit of harmless experimentation to see how it would feel, set all this crap in motion? You thought what about it? That I was homosexual like you because of that innocent moment in time. It was nothing, Luke, nothing. It lasted all of a second or two and that was the last time I ever thought about it."

"LIAR! LIAR!"

Luke erupted into a volcanic rampage overturning furniture and slashing cushions to shreds while swearing a blue streak at Mark the entire time. Mark felt his time was up. Once Luke tired of slashing inanimate objects he would once again turn his attention onto the target of his vengeance. Although Mark deduced some of what might be happening in Luke's twisted brain, why he felt the way he did, Mark still could not comprehend the full picture.

He had only a few fragments of information to go with, nothing conclusive to begin to sort out the incredible complexity of the situation he faced. Something about Luke touching him during a seemingly innocuous moment at primary school had launched him into this tirade of exaggerated proportions. Mark watched in terrified amazement at what he imagined he had looked like with Louise on the atoll. No wonder the poor woman was scared to death. It scared him more than he could admit.

When Luke finally managed to gain some control, he placed himself in front of Mark with pure hatred twisting his features into a mask of foulness and evil, his rancid sweat reeking in the stultifying atmosphere. Growling like an animal, he thumped Mark hard on the knife wound to his thigh. Mark nearly fainted from the sheer agony. Luke then followed up with a fist to the abdomen causing renewed bleeding. He restrained himself from stabbing Mark in the neck, which he lusted for. Luke was salivating at the destruction he caused to his nemesis. Mark's cries of pain were pure music to his ears.

He had waited so long for the moment that he was in raptures, almost dancing on the spot with anticipation of the final act, the climax to his stupendous performance. The last few items of information remained to be revealed. He must calm himself to allow Mark the full experience. Luke resumed his position in the armchair. He needed Mark to hold on to his precious life just a while longer to deliver the coup-de-grace.

"How dare you tell me it was nothing? The defining moment in both our lives and you dare lie about it to me? I was there, shithead, in the showers after everyone left. I knew you stayed longer just to be with me. You knew I was there waiting for you like I always did, devotedly waiting for you to notice me. That day you finally saw me watching you, saw me walking up to you, to help you soap your back the way you let others do. I did it so slowly that day, enjoying every second while I soaped your lovely broad back, your legs and then your bum, right up into the cleft you let me go, enjoying it as much as I did. It was our time, finally, our time to recognise each other for what we were.

"You let me soap your front while I stood behind you growing so hard between my legs. I was never surer of anything in my life than at that moment. It was all so confusing and shameful before that, until you let me hold your cock with my hand while I washed it with the soap, then, I knew. I felt you growing hard too, no way can you deny it, arsehole. I felt it getting hard in my hand. Then…then you just turned off the shower and walked away. Walked out of the shower without a word, dried yourself and acted as if nothing happened, you bastard.

"I followed you for months after that trying to get your attention, trying to be alone with you again but it seemed like you were avoiding me. I decided that you were too embarrassed by your feelings for me to show them, that you were ashamed of what you were as well. It was hard for me to leave you alone, to allow you to sort through your feelings in your own time, but I loved you so much that I knew I had to. Eventually, you would come around and we could finish what we started. I knew we would be together, eventually. I wanted you so badly, I loved you so dearly it hurt to look at you. I grew hard every time I thought back to that day in the shower. I have masturbated so often over that memory that I just about pulled it off.

"Then, at the end of the year, my mother and I had to leave and I never saw you again until that day in the city. I was so happy to see you, you have no idea. You looked even better then, more manly and mature as a university student. God, I almost came in my pants just looking at you. I took you to that bar and then everything changed, didn't it? You looked at me differently, like I was dirt. You didn't even finish your drink. Took your phone call and left me there without the slightest acknowledgment of what you felt, what we meant to one another. I saw the way you looked at my friends. At first, I thought you might have been jealous and a bit angry, but I didn't know why you should be. After all, it was only you that I wanted.

"We never did get back together, did we? No, because you reckoned you were too good for me, didn't you? Ignoring my phone calls, running the opposite direction when I saw you on the street, even catching a tram in the opposite direction of your apartment just to get away from me. I tried to get you a bit jealous by allowing you to see me with other guys, but I saw the look on your face. That was the final straw for me, that look of disgust when you saw me kissing Adam that day on Brunswick Street. I knew then that I would never have you the way I wanted you, that you would deny your true feelings forever. So I watched and waited. I spied on you for years and you never knew.'

"I even paid a private detective to keep tabs on you all through university and your crappy job afterwards. Right up to the time I saw Louise at the railway station that day, upset at seeing you with your sister. I couldn't work out why she would be so upset at seeing you and your sister together.'

"It only took me a short time to get in her good graces to find out, and that was when my plan was hatched. If I couldn't have you, then neither could she. I was going to make you hurt like you hurt me. I had to start a disgusting an affair with her to get her away from you. I nurtured the resentment she had for you thinking you had betrayed her. Nourished her continuing disappointment in you and your endless hours at work, the misery you had become.

"While Louise fell for my charms and my plans, she still harboured lingering feelings for you. She wanted to get back with you which she was going to do on the holiday after you came to your senses. She wanted my help to make you see the error of your ways with a sort of intervention, whereby she and I would make you see the truth.

"I played along with the silly girl. She was pregnant and emotional and I was going to be there to make sure that you two never got together again. Once she hit you with the bombshell of the pregnancy then she would gradually bring you back around to her way of thinking, but I would make sure it didn't happen. You were never going to be with her. NEVER! Neither were you going to be with the brat. The moment I found out about that I had to start planning all over again. No fucking way were you going to have the kid, no fucking way!'

"Luke, I was never going to keep, Louie, surely he told you that?"

"But the little shit wanted to be with you, didn't he? Badgered me about it till I nearly puked. All that horrible gushing sentiment. Fucking little shit had it coming I tell you. I showed him. You and he can see each other in hell maybe, but not in this life."

"Luke, what, what did you do? You didn't… How could you do that to your own son?"

Luke looked momentarily taken aback, confused. He swayed on his feet for a time before he rallied his thoughts. Abruptly, Luke collapsed back into the chair and reclined, absently scratching his chin with the tip of the knife, ruminating on Mark's words. Finally, he smiled a mirthless grin as he once again believed he held information vital to the developing improvisation.

He mulled it over, deciding which direction he should take. He had new ammunition with which to deliver a stunning blow. It had nagged him the entire time since their return. He thought it was a ruse by the two of them to get away with murder. He truly believed it was nothing but a concoction brewed by Mark's clever lawyer mind but he could see now that he was wrong. He could see that the anger he had taken out on the boy for being in league with the devil in front of him wasn't justified after all.

Luke carefully weighed up all he had heard and seen to that point, including everything Mark had said under duress, under fear for his life. He could tell that Mark wasn't lying, he was telling the truth. Luke chuckled to himself as he thought of the implications, of the ramifications once he divulged the story.

Luke was tickled pink at the development. He would see Mark pay so dearly for everything that had transpired, for rejecting him all those years, for making him feel like dirt beneath his feet. Luke's quick mind gathered the information, analysing it and rearranging the scene to utilise it with the greatest proficiency.

"She didn't tell you. You never made it to Hawaii, but she didn't tell you while you were marooned. All that time on the little atoll together and she never told you. Her plan was to get you outrageously jealous, hurt you like she had been hurt. When you reached Hawaii, we were to gang up on you, make you see the light, then reveal the truth. *Her* plan anyway. My plan was to never tell you the truth, but make out that Louise was lying so you could never get back together.

"She obviously played out the first scene on the plane like we discussed, then the bloody thing blew up and I wished so badly that you were dead. She never got to play the second scene at the hotel room that we had planned, the scene where she intended to reveal the truth to you. That she actually still loved you and wanted to resume the marriage preparations if you could forget about the slut she saw you with and quit your job.

"Poor, demented thing. Little did she know what I had planned, that I was going to absolutely fuck it up for both of you. Little did she know that she was going to die anyway from having had sex with me. You see, your rejection saw me falling on rather sad times. Drugs, needles, unsafe sex and so on. I have nothing to lose you see. I am not afraid of killing you or having shut the boy up for good because I'm living a death sentence every day thanks to you.

"The curse of the modern age and all homosexuals and drug addicts. I'm HIV positive. I have it, and so did Louise I'm sure, although she didn't know it. I was secretly hoping that you might have had sex with her again so I could watch you die from it as well. According to Louise, you did, didn't you? You did fuck her once. I know. When Louise fell pregnant she had a procedure to determine possible genetic disorders in the foetus, called an amniocentesis. That test proved more than the absence of abnormalities. You see, both Louise and I are RH negative, but the foetus was RH positive."

Luke lounged back with satisfaction at having delivered the stunning news. Mark, however, stared back at him without comprehension. Luke waited patiently for the penny to drop. He wanted to savour the moment it did. He watched Mark battle with the information as his trembling hands clasped his two wounds, wincing with the discomfort. Luke intended to aid to that discomfort considerably, but not before Mark fully understood the implications of his testimony.

"Don't you see? You asked me how I could harm my own child. I didn't harm my own child, although I'd have no qualms about doing so if it were mine. I harmed *your* child, you fucking idiot. The baby was never my child and both Louise and I knew it all along. No way can two negatives make a positive. You're blood type positive. O positive if I'm not mistaken?

"No, I shut *your* fucking brat up for good with his constant Uncle, Uncle, Uncle. Fucking little shit, I couldn't stand it anymore. Chew on that one you piece of shit. You were never going to see him again anyway, I'm going to kill you because I don't care what happens to me. If I get thrown in jail I'll have all the sex I want until I finally croak it. I probably did your brat a favour, he would most likely have had the disease as well."

Mark sat there calmly mulling over everything. Luke was insane, he knew that, and only half-believed anything he said. That he would harm Louie, of that he was certain. If only in spite, Mark knew that Luke was capable of anything considering the situation. He allowed himself to be completely still, his mind and body, relaxing every sinew, muscle and tendon, lowering his heartbeat to normal, breathing evenly. Mark closed his eyes momentarily as he figured out a possible plan of action. He was unable to come up with anything more plausible than launching himself at Luke in a surprise attack. If he was able to take Luke unawares he might have an advantage, though, in his weakened, wounded state, he seriously doubted his success.

When it happened, it happened as if Mark were in a slow-motion movie scene. With a cool, calm reserve, every motion was calculated and accurate on his part. The lunge forward, the grip on Luke's arm holding the knife. Forcing his weight upon the arm as he plummeted forward to connect his head with Luke's face.

Blood splattered everywhere in a spray of slow-moving droplets bursting from Luke's shattered nose. Luke, letting go of the knife at the moment of impact. Mark, seizing the knife as it began its fall, then plunging it to the hilt, into the centre of Luke's heart. The strength of the thrust near burying the knife in its entirety, into Luke's chest.

Luke barely had sufficient time to call out in surprise before he breathed his last. With his heart no longer functioning, the blood flow gradually ceased, and all was still in a manner of seconds. To Mark, those seconds seemed to last an hour. He collapsed back onto the sofa, spent from the exertion.

With his wounds bleeding profusely once more, Mark broke from his reverie in time to staunch the flow in his thigh with a make-shift tourniquet. He wadded some fabric into his abdomen to soak up the blood flowing freely there, dizzy from the loss. He tied a towel around his waist to keep the wad in place while he sorted through the mental anguish he faced. He desperately tried to wade through the mire of information, attempting to disseminate the truths, from the untruths and half-truths.

Could it possibly be that Louie was his son? Obviously Luke was not the father if what he said could be believed. He didn't know Luke's blood type, or Louie's. He knew that Louise had the rare blood type AB negative. It made her very popular with the blood bank. He knew he was O positive, so if Louie was also of a positive blood group and Luke was telling the truth about being negative, it was possible that Mark was the father.

Small comfort that was, when he faced the prospect that his son no longer lived. Mark gathered his wits, to firstly see to his wounds, which would at the very least, need stitching. He would have to disinfect the wounds as thoroughly as possible but believed he was probably infected by Luke's blood, regardless. He soon realised he could not go see a doctor or go to the hospital. They would recognise it as a knife wound immediately and have to report it. He would not be given bail again once the whole mess was discovered. He would be remanded to jail to await trial on all counts pending, including the death of Luke.

The secret preparations taking up that ten per cent of the spare time would soon come to the fore.

EPILOGUE

Roaring over the Pacific in the twin-hulled vessel with power to burn, trailing a fully laden sailing vessel behind them, Mark once again berated himself for not having the sense to play it cooler. He allowed himself to take another man's life and might live long enough to regret his act of foolishness. While it could be assumed that his uncontrollable rage had taken over his mind at a crucial time, it was, in fact, the exact opposite that occurred. Mark was actually more in control than at any other time in his life. He simply had to get a job done and did it quickly without dramatics.

He needed to punish a person guilty of ruining his life, and the lives of two others. Luke's incomprehensible actions, his premeditated actions, had shaken Mark to the core. Without Luke's intercession, he and Louise may have worked out the misunderstanding at the train station, may have even laughed about it afterwards. Fuelled on by Luke, it was never a consideration.

Mark didn't regret taking Luke's life, never would. He may die a slow and horrible death thanks to Luke's contaminated blood, so he didn't spare a single thought on misgivings. After he patched himself up as best he could, sewing up his wounds with cotton and needle from his sister's sewing kit, Mark left the unit. He borrowed his sister's car to attend to countless details left to be arranged as part of his secret preparations. When everything was done to the best of his abilities in the time he was given before all hell broke loose, Mark returned his sister's car to the unit's garage, leaving a note inside. Mark then had to face his greatest fear before he could embark upon his escape.

Several hours later saw Mark boarding the twin-hulled powerboat packed to overflowing with provisions and extra fuel for the journey ahead. He had intended to go back to sea, to escape the nightmare of their arrival in Australia. He stored the vessel during the preparations at an inlet off the bay in a suburb called Mordialloc. He had passed through the suburb often in his travels around Melbourne and remarked about the quaint inlet to Louise a few times.

There, he spent a lot of time and money on his escape plan. He didn't want to risk his chances in a courtroom. He felt guilty enough about having taken part in Louise's demise to not want to face a jury and prosecution over the matter. He was unable to trust himself not to simply confess to the wrongful death and be done with it.

Mark knew that there was only one option left to him if he couldn't trust himself to defend his case with maximum effort. He had to flee and be certain that no one knew of his plans. He bought the boats under assumed names, paid for the moorings under different names, used several disguises whenever he approached the boats and made sure he was never being followed.

He stowed every conceivable item he thought he may require when spending the rest of his days back at the atoll, if, he could manage to find it. He had many conversations from a public payphone with the trawler captain as to where Mark was found and might possibly have sailed from. He gleaned as much knowledge from the captain as possible about sea currents and prevailing winds at the time of his rescue. There were literally hundreds of possible coral atolls, islets and uninhabited islands dotting the Pacific Ocean between Australia and Hawaii, any one of which may have been his. He had on board a variety of detailed sea charts with up to date information.

It didn't matter if he didn't find the same place. He had on board, enough provisions, tools, seeds and livestock to begin from scratch on a more suitable island. The choices of habitable islands were plentiful to anyone willing to expend the energy required to locate one. Mark's plan was simply to motor on in the powerboat until his fuel ran out, then reverse the order of vessels. He would sail his other boat, towing the motorboat until he found what he was looking for.

Mark sighed heavily as the consequences of his actions took their toll on his psyche. His nerves were strung as taut as piano wire, had been from the moment the police questioned him about Louise. Worst of all was Luke's revelations about Louie and about what Luke had done to the boy. That was the catalyst that finally drove Mark over the edge.

His mad rush to Luke's home in the outer suburbs near Frankston, to find Louie's bloody body tied up and gagged in a closet was the end for Mark. He could no longer keep it together from that moment on. He knew he had only a small window of opportunity in which to return to his boat, to strike out on his journey beyond the bay to open sea without being spotted by authorities. He planned to leave close on dusk and navigate purely by chart, compass and sat nav.

He had taken a rudimentary course in navigation via the internet, giving him a rough understanding of the process, although he didn't have a sextant with which to pinpoint his exact location. He purchased the latest satellite navigation system he could find via the internet. He wanted to leave behind as few traces of his purchasing evidence as possible. Therefore, he purchased everything under an alias with all goods to be delivered to a bogus address, that of an abandoned house several blocks away from Brianna's apartment.

He took a very real risk that the packages would either not be delivered or left by the post, or that they might be stolen, but it was a risk he had to take. He wanted to give authorities the least possible chance of locating him. He managed to stay hidden for nearly ten years, he supposed he could remain undetected for as long as he had left.

He held no hopes that he had avoided blood contamination by Luke's blood mixing with his open wounds. When Mark broke Luke's nose his diseased blood sprayed everywhere all at once, including Marks wounds. He was under no false impressions that he may have escaped the death threat posed by the incurable disease plaguing the twenty-first century. He had been given a death sentence which he intended to serve back on the atoll. It was as good a place as any to live out his days. He could think of many worse ways, and places, to do so, including a maximum-security prison back in Australia. If he died sooner of other causes then so be it. He stockpiled as many medical supplies as he could, including antibiotics. Enough to see off most normal infections and general ailments. Common flu and the like were not envisaged by living on a clean atoll with no other human contact from the mainland. So all was as good as it was going to get he felt.

"Will we find it?"

"Maybe, maybe not. I can only give it my best shot."

"Thank-you."

"What for?"

"For everything. For what you did. For coming for me."

"I had no choice, Louie. I had to find out what he did to you. Thank Christ, he didn't kill you, at least not straight away anyway. You do realise that you could have the disease as well? You do understand that, don't you?"

"Yes, Uncle…dad."

"Even if I didn't find out you were my son, I would still have come for you, Louie. I had to know, had to find out for myself. I guess the police would have found you in time once they discovered Luke's body at the landfill in Clayton, but I doubt it. You were pretty banged up and hardly breathing because of the swelling in your throat and nose when I found you. Louie, I have to tell you, it was the happiest moment of my life when I saw you alive in that closet. I firmly believed he had killed you but my heart just wouldn't let my mind accept it. How are you feeling by the way?"

"I feel great um...dad. Better now that we're going back home. I never wanted to leave, but I supposed you were right about a lot of things. I don't blame you for what happened, and I'm really glad you did that to him. He wasn't a nice person, he hated me because of you."

"I know you don't blame me, Louie but I still feel as guilty as hell for taking you away from your home to face that nightmare. In a way, I made things a lot worse than they should have been because I was feeling so guilty about your mother. If I had lawyered up properly, I could have talked my way out of all those charges. It probably wouldn't have stopped Luke from going postal on us, though. He was one freaky, whacked-out, son-of-a-bitch. Regardless of what happens, regardless of whether you are my son or not, Louie, I love you. I want you to know that. I love you with all my heart and I am glad I was dumped into the middle of the Pacific Ocean if that's what it took for us to be together and for me to finally realise that."

The End

Other Titles by Josef Peeters:
Fiction

DAINTREE DENIZENS

When Barry Ottoman's idyllic, solitary, lifestyle is shattered
by the appearance of interlopers with a mysterious agenda and
intent on harm, he must call upon his vast knowledge of Australia's
northern rainforest's flora and fauna, to effect an escape from a
deadly pursuit.
Purchase links available on Josef's website;
https://lakesidecaravanpark.wixsite.com/josef

TRANSIENCE

Ephemeral images from a troubling dream inspire Samuel Border to meet a girl who proceeds to capture his heart. The transience of their encounter in no way reflects the indelible imprint haunting his mind, but events intervene to postpone their union. A compulsion to locate the woman of his dreams results in a tragic accident to his younger brother, causing Samuel to abandon the search. Only happenstance many years later alters that decision.

Were life simply about the present and not unduly influenced by an evil family legacy, Samuel would not be drawn inexorably toward his destiny. It will require all his instincts and courage to bring the woman he loves beyond measure home safely.

Purchase links available on Josef's website;
https://lakesidecaravanpark.wixsite.com/josef

MT. MOULAMEIN

Something is dreadfully wrong in the small, outback town of Moulamein, Australia. Something so profoundly unsettling that Chris Hall, a fugitive, hiding out in the most unlikely of places, faces the daunting responsibility of informing the town residents of the truth. Even convincing his childhood sweetheart, Carly Parish is a mission fraught with peril and often, death. The improbable truth, revealed only by evading the midnight signal, will not set them free. It will take the cooperation of many highly differing cultures to produce a plan with which to survive the impending disaster threatening their town and so much more.

Purchase links available on Josef's website;
https://lakesidecaravanpark.wixsite.com/josef

BLACK HEART

When a gruesome murder shocks the small cane farming community of Ingham, Queensland, Detective Arnold Ryan feels it more keenly than most, since the victim is an old friend. Ryan's vow to apprehend the culprit intensifies when a second incident, bearing all the trademarks of the first, leaves another friend dead.

Realising his prime suspect has cause to hate him and his friends, Ryan must act quickly to prevent further bloodshed. Moreover, an escalation by the serial killer may uncover a dark secret that the township--and Ryan--would rather leave buried.

Purchase links available on Josef's website;
https://lakesidecaravanpark.wixsite.com/josef

ABOUT THE AUTHOR

Josef arrived in Australia with his parents and siblings in 1964. A near lifetime of creative pursuits has culminated in his desire to produce entertaining stories. Josef lives with his wife in the tiny outback town of Moulamein, NSW Australia where they own and manage a small caravan park, while they each indulge in their artistic endeavours. Josef chooses to base his stories in Australian settings, populating them with authentic-sounding Aussie characters. While this approach will not appeal to everyone, he stays true to the country he has grown to love.

www.ingramcontent.com/pod-product-compliance
Lightning Source LLC
Chambersburg PA
CBHW071518100726
47908CB00004B/1212